WINTER AT HORNBLOOD

EPIC OF HORNBLOOD CASTLE #2

ERIC KERCHER

PAPER AND SWORD, LLC

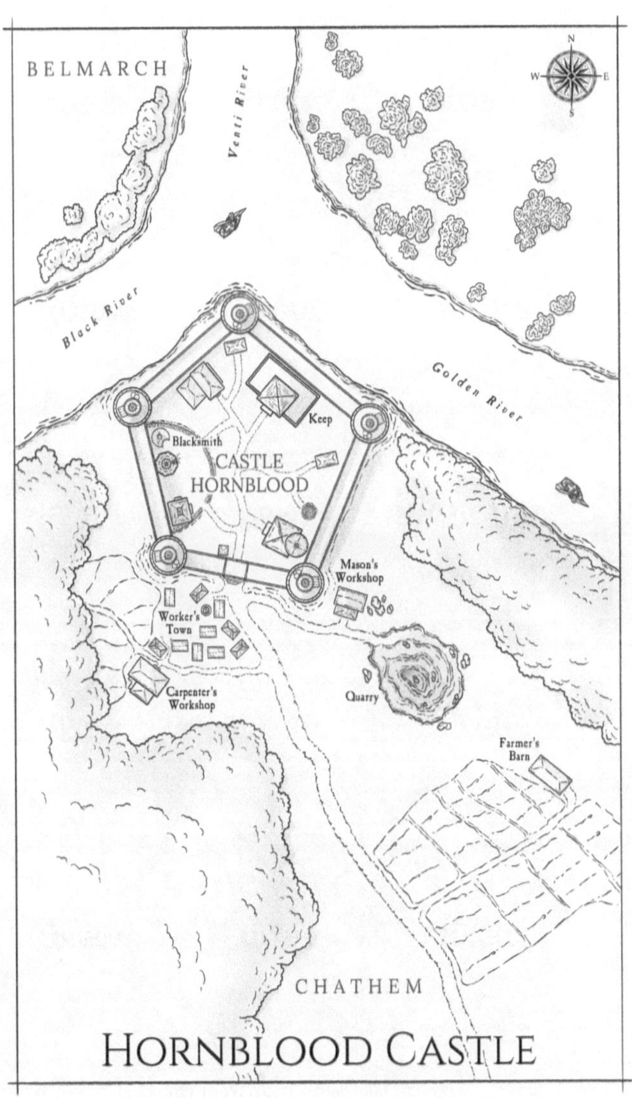

HORNBLOOD CASTLE

To Milo

From the Author

There are days when we all need an escape from a terrible job, a terrible day, or a terrible life.

Join my newsletter and get an escape from the real world, stories, and lore designed to entertain and delight.

You'll also get *Stories from the Deep*, an exclusive, unpublished anthology chock full of extra epilogues, short stories, and lore from the Patmos Sea Fantasy Adventure Series.

Join now at erickercher.com.

Enjoy the book.

-Eric Kercher

1

Fog of Wine

"Still there?" Ned joined Sam on the wall, staring out over the bloodstained field. Winter was around the corner, the winds turning cold and biting when the sun went down. Leaves were falling now, most of the gold, brown, and red coating the forest floor.

"Still there." Sam pulled at his coat, itching his bandages. A few days hadn't done much to heal them. "Shouldn't you be asleep?"

"I should be asking you the same question." Ned's beard and mustache had grown out, just as bushy, if not more so, than his eyebrows. They couldn't hide the gauntness of his cheeks, though.

"Give me a few minutes, I'll be in. Any word from Overseer Rhys?" There was another question to that, deeper.

"That's your realm, not mine."

Captain Yand had left a deep hole, one that Sam hoped the young Duke would fill. So far, though...

"He's young, give him time." *Not that young.* Twenty was more than old enough to be a journeyman apprentice, if not a full carpenter.

The thought reminded him of Archie. His gaze was pulled over to the freshly mounded sections of earth in the corner of the castle. That, Overseer Rhys had done well to execute. The ceremony had been short, the mourners few, but the entire castle had been there. Duke Hornblood included.

Forty-seven. Forty-seven men remained alive within the walls to man and fight. Another thirty-five women and children on top of that.

A heron skimmed along the tree line, then dipped into the river beyond. It was far outside of their line of sight now.

"I'll go inside." Sam stood up, aches and pains twitching at him. Ned clapped him on the shoulder, which brought a sting with it.

"Sorry. Get some rest."

The fires of the Belmarch burned well beyond the arrow range of their bows. Sam had hoped they would give up without a leader, that they would slink back across the river in the dead of the night one day. That hadn't happened. Now, he doubted it ever would.

They had burned their dead on pyres, the bodies that they could. Sam had ordered the others dumped into the river. The pillars that had gone up then were big, and white. The fires burned hot, consumed everything, including flesh and bone. *Whatever they believed, their dead were gone, just like ours.*

Sam limped down the stairs, feeling a pang in his left foot every time he set it down, but eventually made it to the bottom. He went back into the Keep, only to find Bill leaning against the wall, waiting for him.

"Sam," Bill said. Sam was startled by the interruption and almost dropped the door on himself.

"Yes?"

"May we... talk?"

Sam nodded, and Bill went back out with him, back across the yard and into his stone hut. The room was cool, warmer than the outside air, but not by much. Bill offered a chair and

Sam took it, sighing as the weight came off his left foot. The small fireplace tucked into one wall was barren and dusty. A spiderweb was strung along one corner. Even Bill couldn't escape the lack of fuel and wood, a prudent rule set by the Overseer. With winter coming, though...

"We need to break free of this siege," Bill said.

"We're in agreement." A long silence stretched between them. Sam was wary. He didn't trust Bill yet. "What do you propose?"

"Kill them all." Bill shrugged. "They won't leave on their own."

The shack smelled of mildew. The floor was damp somehow, even though they hadn't had rain in a while, near the fireplace. Sam shifted in the chair to get more comfortable, easing the way it was digging into his back.

"Easier said than done." His voice was full of sarcasm.

"You know the Duke isn't cut out for this." Bill shook his head. "I don't know where he's been hiding his stash of booze, but I'd love to know where." He licked his lips. "Loves it more than I ever did."

Sam looked into his eyes, the strange look of truthfulness in them. *Was that true, or was it just what he believed?*

"We can't force him to act."

"We have to." Bill pointed out his window. "Or do you want to die here? They'll tear us limb from limb and feed us to the dogs if they could."

He jabbed at the large bandages wrapped around his torso. "Or did you forget the man who gave you that?"

Sam frowned. Mention of it made his wound burn and itch. It hurt, but only grazed his ribcage. "I remember."

"He would have broken you earlier, had he not wanted to toy with you, make you an example."

"He's dead now," Sam reminded him.

"But another will rise in his place."

"How do you know so much about the Belmarch?" Sam squinted at him, examining his face, his hands.

"I've lived near the border all my life. It's impossible not to know them." Bill leaned in closer. "If you did, you'd hate them like I do."

Sam didn't see where this was going, and the look in Bill's eyes made him uncomfortable. The man was small and wiry, but somehow he had managed to escape the fight with a few cuts and scratches. And Trent said he was covered in blood. How he managed to do that, Sam had a burning desire to know, but at the same time didn't.

"We can agree on all of this," Sam sat back. "So, what does it have to do with me?" He crossed his arms.

"You're a fighting man, but not just any fighting man." Bill leaned in more. "You could take control, lead us out of this place."

"That sounds an awful lot like a revolt."

"Revolt? No. Such a strong word. Such a dirty word." Bill held up his hands, as if innocent. "You're not just a fighter, are you?"

"I've seen my share of bloodshed. I want to put it behind me, to leave it where it belongs. No man should kill another."

"Come now, Sam. We both know better. Men must die, either by another man's hands or of old age. Why is it that certain men keep the privilege for themselves?"

"Is that what the Belmarch think? That any man can kill another?" There was something wrong in the words. Twisted, perverted. They made so much sense, but didn't feel right.

A child yelled in the courtyard. It made Sam stop, but the sound of laughter followed, and he relaxed.

"I want to survive just as badly as any other man, but there are some things I'll not do."

Bill's eyes watched him, dark and foreboding. "We'll see how well you keep that word."

Sam stood up, unable to be in the man's presence anymore. "I take my leave of you." His voice was gruff and short. Bill nodded but said nothing.

An unpleasant man. Always had been, always will be. Sam was glad to shut the door behind him, even though the day had faded into twilight and brought with it more chill.

How long had it been? A few months? A few weeks? Weariness overtook him, burrowing deep into his bones. Everything seemed to blend together. He went to bed troubled, not seeing a way forward, no path of survival.

"How do you propose we do that?" Evan took another sip. He turned the goblet in his hand, examining it in the failing light. It was dirty, smudged with fingerprints, and streaked. That was what he could see, in better light he suspected it would be worse. It smelled better than it looked, the aroma of the dark, red wine pleasantly floral. Better than the smell of death and blood, or the commoners that stunk.

"I still have some pull in the capital." Overseer Rhys sat across from him. "Provided I can get to them, there are those who would still listen to me."

He was fat, but not as much as he used to be. Evan's stomach grumbled, but he ignored it. Wine would help with that, too.

"Do you have an army that can sally forth and break a hole in the invader's ranks? Or perhaps a secret passage you've been hiding from me that goes straight to the King's chambers?" Duke Evan rubbed his eyes. He wearied of this topic, which had come up more frequently since...He was gone.

Through the buzz in his head, he knew that. He wished he were still here now, standing beside him with that disappointed look.

"No..." The Overseer shifted in his seat.

"Then let us speak of it no more." He was tired and lonely. Even the Overseer was too far below his rank to be called a friend in this place. Even a cousin would be better than nothing. He'd even take Theo, brash and stupid as he was, for a companion than rot away here.

The Overseer clearly wanted to talk more of it, but he cleared his throat and took out a scrap of parchment. "Shall we proceed to inventory, then?"

Evan cringed. "Go on."

"Barrels of flour, thirty-two. Barrels of biscuit, fifteen. Boxes of nails, ten. Quarried stone, fifteen thousand pieces..." The Overseer went down his list, order unchanged from last time. Food continued to decrease, as did everything else.

He droned on. Evan drank more, then emptied his goblet. He thought about filling it up, but the long list was making him sleepy.

Then something caught his attention.

"Casks of wine, three. Bottles of wine, seventeen."

Evan sat up. "Stop. What was that?"

The Overseer licked his lips, wrinkled his brow, and went over his list again. "Oak, seven stacks?"

"The wine."

"Ah. Three casks, seventeen bottles."

"I thought we had over twenty bottles last week." His heart palpitated. It didn't sound bad until he thought back to the first inventory. Double the casks and over a hundred bottles of his own personal stock had accompanied him here.

The Overseer's mouth was working, but no sound came out.

"Answer me," he said.

"We did, sire."

"Then who took it?" Another long pause.

"Wine has only been issued to your Highness."

"What? No." He ran through the week in his head. There was no way he had drunk that much wine. Or was there?

His head buzzed, and he stood up and went to the bar with the bottle. It was almost empty. He opened the case up with his key. A quick count confirmed it, then another count. Seventeen bottles, standing like sentinels.

"It can't be. Someone has been stealing from me."

"Sire—"

"I don't want excuses, Rhys, I want answers. Find the man that did this and bring him to me." He drained the bottle into his goblet. Half a glass, at best. It tasted sickly sweet.

"I will conduct an investigation," the Overseer's eyes drooped. "And I will report all that I can find."

"Good. Carry on." The wine went to his head, made him feel drowsy. The long list of supplies didn't help. He wasn't paying attention, even long after the Overseer had concluded and tucked away his paper. He was thinking about his father and uncle. What would they do if they were in his situation? Would they ride out, breastplate burnished and gleaming, to lead a fatal charge and break the enemy line? Or would they do what he was doing, hide away here in the safety of his walls and wait for the inevitable to happen?

He cursed his luck, and his own stupidity for pushing his father to send him, and for Yand for not stopping him.

Even through the fog of the wine he knew that wasn't quite right. The memory of that night came back, the low conversation, Yand imploring him to wait until the castle was finished. But he had pushed for this, to distinguish himself and prove his mettle.

He stared into the goblet. Was this all he could do? Was this his character?

The Overseer stared at him. Evan realized he had been calling his name for some time.

"Yes?"

"What are your orders, sire?"

His orders? His orders? A spark of anger tried to ignite, but it found nothing inside him to burn. Instead, it smoldered. Evan looked upon Rhys with contempt. What right did he have to demand from Duke Hornblood?

"I grow tired." His speech was starting to slur. "Leave me."

The Overseer clamped his mouth shut and stood. He gathered his robes. "Goodnight, your Highness."

He left. Evan stood in front of his desk, staring up at the crest of his family as tears rolled down his cheek.

2

MEMORIES OF THE DEAD

Swords, axes, and knives were spread out over the floor. Sam rubbed his chin.

"This is what we got?"

"That's everything." Mathew knelt down and touched one of them. The barracks were dark and musty. Dirt was strewn everywhere on the floor, and the beds were unmade.

Sam recalled helping to make some of them a long time ago. It seemed so distant now, even though it had to have been less than a year.

"And what are you going to do with them?"

"That's just it. We don't really know." Mathew stood up and shrugged. He had aged years in the last few weeks. "I didn't know who else to go to."

"You should take them to the Overseer. Have him decide."

"We talked about that..." Mathew dropped his gaze to the floor. Something felt off, but he didn't know what.

He wished he was still in bed sleeping, that the young boy hadn't come to get him. He wished the head guard hadn't been killed in the fighting, leaving a vacant hole for someone to fill.

And, he realized, he knew who they had in mind.

"I'm a carpenter, not a leader."

"We keep the watches, rotate them like we used to. How long will that last?" Mathew shook his head, then grabbed onto his arm. "I'm afraid of the others sometimes, the look in their eyes. Hopelessness."

Sam took a deep breath, then let it out. He told the truth—he was no leader. What experience did he have guarding a castle?

Nights on the picket line tickled the back of his mind, but he thrust them away.

"Pick the man most willing to lead. That's my advice to you."

"Right now, that's me, and I can't do it. I haven't led anything, let alone the defenses of a castle."

The man most able to do that task lay in a grave not a stone's throw from where they were talking. Funny, how life ended up like that.

What authority did he have, though? Just because Mathew thought he was more suited? A man half his age determining the course of the leadership?

Sam couldn't help but let his mind wander back to his conversation with Bill. It had put him on edge, and here Mathew was doing just about the same.

"Talk to the Overseer. He'll know what to do."

"I can't. I'm just a guard, and everyone else is the same. The rejects that couldn't make it in the capital, sent to the boundaries of the kingdom." His eyes were filled with anguish.

"You've survived a battle. You can survive this." Sam patted him on the shoulder, intending to slip away. He had lingered here too long.

"At least come with me. To give me courage and a kind word?"

Kindness isn't what the Overseer showed him. "I don't think that would be a good idea..."

"Please?" It was worse than a cat crying over spilled milk, and almost as pitiable.

He wanted to shake him, to tell him he was a grown man and he needed to fight his own battles. To leave him out of it.

But how can I do that?

"I'll go with you then," Sam said reluctantly.

The relief on Mathew's face made it seem like a good decision.

"Thank you. Thank you from the bottom of my heart." He shook his head. "I've lost so much sleep thinking about this."

Sleep. That was one thing they all needed more of. It seemed like the entire castle was on a knife's edge, everyone underfed and tired. He hadn't realized it until just then.

"When we get out of this, everyone will sleep a lot better." Sam wanted to get out of the barracks, uncomfortable in the cold, unpleasant room. The smells, the taste of sharp iron. He wanted to leave. "Come get me when you're ready. I need to get to the workshop to start the day."

"Can you go now?" The question stuck into him, unanticipated.

He wasn't ready to go now. "I have to meet Kerien to get him started on a new idea I've had," Sam said. "I couldn't be done until next afternoon."

"Afternoon would be good. It will give me the morning to gather my wits. Will you meet me after lunch?"

Sam searched for an excuse. A task, watch? Mathew would know his watch schedule. That wouldn't work.

"That will do fine." Sam edged to the door. A visibly happier Mathew walked him to it.

"I'll be ready. You don't know how much this means to me and everyone else."

Troubled, Sam left the young man. He wasn't sure there wouldn't be a revolt if the Overseer did what he wanted and clapped him in chains.

Cool, distant. That encompassed every interaction Sam had had with him lately, ever since the attack and Yand's death.

He wondered what the man had been doing. What had he been scheming, whispering in the Duke's ear?

The cool winds of late autumn blew across the courtyard, capturing his coat and threatening to pull it off. If it could be called a coat. It was a collection of rags now, cobbled together from garments of dead men.

The others were already there as he entered. Trent and Kerien were splitting arrows, and Ned, looking even more tired than Mathew had, was shaping a new bow.

"Where have you been?" Kerien asked sharply.

"Mind yourself," Sam said. The storm cloud in his heart darkened, threatening to break. Kerien narrowed his eyes, but held his tongue.

Sam felt some pity for him, his leg bandaged up like that.

However, the attitude it gave him was more than enough to quash the feeling.

The comforting smells of wood dust and oil of the workshop helped though. After the outburst, everyone busied themselves with their work, at least until things calmed down again.

Sam went to his workbench and put his hands on it, resting and feeling its weight. He had spent many an hour here, and it was an old, familiar friend. The smooth top was worn and dinged by countless projects, the shelf beneath filled with offcuts and chunks of special wood, even the way it creaked when he leaned against it. It all helped center him in a time of madness.

While he listened to the others work, scraping, cutting, and polishing away, he wondered what it would have been like to lose this too.

So much had been burned in the first attack. His clothes, his shack, even the letters he had been saving. The one, single reminder of his old life had disappeared in ash and smoke. Drifted away, never to return.

In some ways, it was a blessing. Now, he could never go back.

Ned cleared his throat and glanced back. Sam was calm enough now, balanced again. *I need to control myself better.*

"Any word on the guard duty?"

"Nothing."

"What did they ask of you?" Trent was focused on his work, even though he wasn't cutting out another shaft for arrows.

What did they ask of me? To entreat for them, or to spark an outburst?

"They had a question about inventory. I told them I couldn't help them and directed them to the Overseer." All true, but not all the truth.

"Too dumb to count anything. Sounds like our guards," Kerien said. He was moping, taking too long with his work. Another thing to irritate Sam, and he knew it.

"With so few of them left they probably feel the strain all too sharply." Ned took up a handful of sand and rubbed it along a high spot on his bow. "Word is they're recruiting, if you'd like to join them."

Kerien snorted. "Never in a million years would I be caught as a guard."

"There are worse occupations."

"Sure, and there are dirtier pigs in a pigpen, but you don't see me digging in one."

"Our young friend has a way with words," Sam said, winking at Ned. He still wanted to knock Kerien upside his head, but would play along for the moment.

"Aye, but you might see him sleeping in one."

Kerien reddened at the comment. Sam shot Ned a questioning look, but he only returned one with a look of mirth.

Kerien said something under his breath, but not loud enough for anyone to hear. Sam had the vague impression it was aimed at Ned, from the way he looked over at his corner of the workshop.

"Why do we have to fight?" Trent was quiet, but there was a will in his voice that shocked the room.

It was so quiet they could have heard a feather drop.

Trent turned, his face screwed up into a strange expression. "Don't we have enough to think about that we shouldn't be fighting?"

"You're right," Ned said softly.

Sam reflected on this in the silence. Things had been so hard since Archie died. His tools were a constant reminder of him.

And a constant reminder that any one of them could be next.

He was right. It hurt that Sam hadn't seen it earlier, hadn't said something earlier. They were at each other's throats, even though they were surrounded by an enemy army.

Sam couldn't help but hang his head in shame. "We've been together for a long time now," he said when the silence had stretched to the breaking point. "If we work together, we'll make it through this. I know it."

"Like Archie made it?" Kerien asked. His face was away from them, engrossed in his workbench.

What do I say to that? Sam couldn't lie, and turned over words in his mouth. All of them seemed to be empty, all of them insufficient.

Should he comfort them, tell them that everything was going to be all right in the end?

He didn't believe that. It might be possible, yes, but to promise it was another sort of matter.

His mind drifted to the dead. To Archie, and the family he loved so much, left behind. To Yand, how hard and uncompromising he had been, but for good reason.

Forcing him to bear his weight had been a reminder to Sam of his own duty. There were those here that needed him, that relied on someone to lead them.

He felt ashamed. Once again, here he was, cowardly and refusing to do what was right. How many would have survived if he had trained with Yand? Something about it made him sick inside. It coiled in his stomach, made its way to his back, and twisted around him. Archie would have been here, and his son would still have a father.

Sam set down his plane, unused. "We have failed Archie. We haven't remembered what he did."

He undid his apron and hung it on the side of his workbench. "Come, everyone. This can wait. We have more important things to do."

He had put others to rest before, but never like this. Men who had fought and died, spilled their blood on the field of battle.

"Where are we going?" Trent asked, his eyes wide and following Sam across the room.

Sam didn't answer, but threw aside the threadbare flap of burlap that functioned as a pitiful wall.

They set down their tools and left tasks unfinished. Ned was first, then Trent, and finally Kerien.

Something was bothering him. It had to, how his eyes were downcast and his jaw shifted.

"Leave it behind," Sam said. "For the moment, at least." Kerien paused, then limped along.

Sam got back in lead, shoulder to shoulder with Ned.

The courtyard was alive with children, but they didn't play as hard as they used to. Their voices were softer and cracked. Thin arms and legs replaced the plump, full frames they used to have.

The boy who had taken his message watched them. Sam smiled at him, and he held up a hand to wave.

Around the back of the Keep and up to the makeshift cemetery, they traveled in silence.

They formed a line around his spot, a bit of wood stuck at the head of the grave.

Others bore similar indications of their trades, mostly stone.

Sam remembered. He remembered the bright smile, the skillful hand. How he used to shave too much on the right side and skew his boards. It had taken him months to correct it, but Archie persisted.

"He was a father, a husband, and a friend." Sam's voice echoed off the hard stone of the wall, shattering and cracking. "A steady hand, a keen eye. Goodbye, Archie, and thank you for everything."

Sam knelt and put his hand on the grave, trembling with a rage and wave of emotion. He crushed the sandy earth between his fingers.

The others did the same, and together they bade a friend farewell.

3

Changes

"We take them at the pass, cut off all retreat to the north." A whisper in the back, a tremor in the front. General Granb's hand traced along the mountain range. "It's a perfect place for an ambush, and they'll never see us coming."

"That's because we can't get there. The roads are already almost blocked, and the mountains are impassable at this time of the year."

"How dare you interrupt, you miserable whelp," Granb said, eyes narrowing and hand on his sword.

Raltone watched in silence, sizing up the situation. Sable wouldn't say anything if he wasn't completely sure of himself.

The young man strode forward, a sneer on his face and his chest out proud. His black hair streamed down his back. "Your time is through, General." His title was dripping with contempt. "And your tactics outdated. I have a better plan."

General Granb turned to Raltone. "Surely you won't listen to this impudent imp?"

"General Granb has driven the unbelievers from their strongholds," Raltone said. The General smiled and turned back. "However, you may proceed." He lifted his little finger.

He had grown too used to leading the men. Whatever Sable's plan, just having it voiced would help bring down the General's ego, and any potential plans for betrayal.

The smirk on Sable's face broadened. He wasn't the most likable man, but his fighting prowess was too valuable to throw away.

He snapped his fingers. At once, the candles in the tent flickered, then some went out.

Raltone couldn't explain it. There they were, flickering and sputtering, doing their best they could to put out their light, but nothing came.

Instead, a gloomy darkness fell over them, and everyone fell into a hush.

"We've bickered and quarreled amongst ourselves for too long." He seemed to grow. From behind the crowd something stirred. Men moved out of the way as an old, wizened figure stepped through them. "But there is another power, an ancient power that has been long forgotten."

The man shuffled to the center of the room and stood next to the map table.

He was entirely unimpressive, but somehow Raltone's eyes were drawn to him. He sat up when the old man produced a shriveled hand from his robe.

"Watch, and see what future awaits us." Sable knelt before the man, who touched him with his finger.

Strange sounds came out of the man's mouth, and the air seemed to suck out of the tent. Raltone sat up, feeling something run up his back.

Sable... *changed*. There was no other way to describe it.

Raltone couldn't look away. Sable seemed to be writhing with pain or pleasure, but the old man chanted on.

Finally, it was done, and Raltone looked upon the man and saw the future incarnate.

When they had made their peace and said their final good-byes, the group of carpenters went back into the workshop, took up their aprons and tools, and stood at their workbench-es.

But none of them put tool to wood.

Even the familiar feel of his favorite chisel, warm and smoothed, with a touch of coolness at the blade, couldn't drive Sam to put it to use.

There was a feeling of hopelessness that hung in the air, more prominent now that Sam could put a finger on it.

He had felt it before, but hadn't recognized it until now.

"What are we going to do?" Trent asked.

The sound shattered the stillness and encompassed every-thing Sam was thinking and feeling.

What are we going to do?

None of them had a family to go to. They didn't have orders from the Overseer to fulfill. Nothing drove them to do anything.

"I'm afraid we wait," Sam said at last, setting down his chisel. His heart wasn't in it, not right now. "Take the rest of the day off. Rest. Relax. Sleep."

It was the sensible thing to do, but they resisted. True, they took off their aprons and put up their tools, but they all lingered.

Sam didn't blame him, he wanted to stay too. To be around people.

Where else could he go? They were trapped within the walls of the castle now. A few hundred yards in any direction would bring them up against an obstacle of stone feet thick.

He felt hot. He was trapped, stuck like a rat in a box. His eyes burned and his neck was on fire.

Sam took a deep breath, suppressing the panic that tried to overtake him. He didn't know what to do. He had never been in this situation, but he wasn't about to lose his head to it.

That would never do, and it wouldn't help at all.

So what was he to do?

He remembered the night in the Duke's chamber, going over plans and constructions. It had been a time of hope, a time of planning.

Perhaps it was time to resurrect those plans, to make his ideas come to life.

Sam turned back to the courtyard. There was plenty of stone left piled in heaps along the wall, but he knew there was little in the way of wood.

His eyes rested on the half-finished keep. It went up two stories, with the third partially complete in two separate watchtowers. They were rounded and projected above the top of the Keep, a place for defenders to rain down arrows if they needed to.

The crane stood lonely, like a lone sentry on the unfinished tower. It hadn't been used in weeks, since the initial attack had halted all construction on the tower. It was still functional, though, and could be used again.

Sam shook his head, remembering the days of sweat and effort that stretched into the long summer days. The work that had gone into that building was overwhelming. Dozens of masons, the carpenters, and the blacksmiths had all helped to make it rise from the dust.

And, with a few tweaks, they might be able to make something of a defense.

But it would take a lot of work. And he would need help.

A leaf fluttered up over the southern wall and twisted in the light breeze. All the trees had shed theirs, leaving the forest bare.

The leaf twirled and danced, then fell into the courtyard to join the few other strays that had come over the wall.

Just like he had. A transplant in a dangerous situation. The fresh smell of the air couldn't help him feel better, and he'd never felt more alone in his life than that time in the makeshift graveyard.

The Overseer was back, standing politely in front of his desk. "What is it?"

"Our daily meeting, sire," he frowned, somewhat ruffled from his normal appearance.

Evan peered out of bloodshot eyes and eyelids that felt too heavy. His head swam. How much had he had to drink?

Two bottles lay empty on the desk before him, and sunlight streamed in the window. The air was stale, and suffocating.

"Already?" It had seemed like hours had passed in a second. Their last meeting had been yesterday, but it felt like the same day.

He smelled bad, and he knew it, but he tried to not be hurt by the way the Overseer's nose wrinkled as he came closer.

Both of him.

"Shall we begin?" He took a seat.

Something in the way he said it made something inside Duke Hornblood snap.

"No."

"Your Highness?"

"No. I'm not ready. I want you to leave, to leave me alone." He clutched at his goblet. It was empty.

He wished it were full, but knew he couldn't handle another drop.

He should be coming up with plans.

He should be walking among his people.

He should be a leader.

Instead, he was here, wallowing in his own filth and drink like a commoner.

How he longed to go back to those days of carousing—staying out late, laughing with the rough and hardy, kissing beautiful women.

Instead, he was here, in the middle of nowhere, surrounded by Belmarch with no hope of prevailing.

"Perhaps in a few hours?" The Overseer was standing now. If he detested the Duke, he didn't show it.

"Curse your hours. Curse your meetings and your supplies and everything else." Evan snatched up the empty goblet and hurled it at him.

The Overseer flinched, but the glass flew well clear of him.

It smashed against the wall, leaving a strange streak to run down the wooden panel.

Anger turned to anguish. Evan stood. "Why do you—" he swayed, the world turning dangerously. He smashed his eyelids together, then opened them wider and clutched at the desk. "Why do you bother me with these trifles? Go train the men."

The desk held him up, if barely, through the outburst. Evan knew he was shouting but didn't care.

He wasn't like his father, strong and stoic, who could turn a man with a soft word. He wasn't like Yand, who didn't need to say anything. Men would snap to attention if he merely walked by.

The Overseer was sweating. "I can't, sire. I don't know how. I'm a courtier, a member of the court, not a fighting man. I haven't picked up a sword in years."

"But you have used a sword." Evan released one hand and pointed it at him, but the motion threw off his balance and he tumbled to the floor.

His head hit the floor with a thud, and pain lanced through his head. Duke Hornblood groaned.

"Your Highness, are you hurt?" Two Overseers swam in his vision.

"Of course I'm hurt, you buffoon." Hands clutched at him, pulling him into a sitting position. He braced his hand on the cold stone.

How long had it been since he had a fire going? A cheering, crackling fire that spit its heat into the room?

Too long.

His head hurt, a dull thumping at the back where he had struck the floor. All his anger was gone. He didn't mind the Overseer helping him into a sitting position.

"I don't know what I'm doing, Rhys," he moaned. "I'm not my father."

"This is true," the Overseer said in a measured tone. He swept the hair from his forehead, looking for blood. "And you aren't Captain Yand."

"Then what am I to do?"

"Be your own man. Be Duke Evan Hornblood, protector of the north and defender of the realm."

"I don't know if I can do it." A momentary vision of himself in full armor, astride Charger, marching into the capitol in victory.

It faded, lost in the gloom of the room. He held out a hand to the sunlight, trying to catch the shaft of yellow.

He would never have that glory. Not in this life. Not now.

Not trapped in here.

"I'm fine." He snatched his hand back into a fist. His head was starting to throb, whether it was the blow or the drink, he knew not. "But we'll have to do this another time."

"I've seen your promise," the Overseer stared at the corner of the room. "I see what your father sees in you."

"My father sees nothing but a disappointment when he looks at me," Evan said bitterly. "A failure. He'll be glad to be rid of me here."

"I don't want to contradict you, sire," the Overseer said softly, "but that is not what your father sees when he looks at you."

The crest stared at him, mocked him. It told the tale of his family, how they grew from nothing to the most powerful clan and vessel liege to the King. They almost single-handedly put him on the throne.

Nothing like him. Nothing like him at all.

The dregs of the night seemed to swirl inside him, sending the world spinning.

He didn't feel well. It was a familiar feeling, one that often led him to strange bedfellows. Like pigs.

What would his father do in this situation? Alone, out-manned, and trapped. Would he lead the host forth in battle? Or would he do something else?

"If you'll excuse me." The Overseer stood and made for the door.

Evan didn't want him to go all of a sudden. It would leave him alone. All alone, like he had always been. No friend, no playmate. Always the Duke and the Grand Duke's son.

"Goodnight, Duke." The door shut with a click.

He was alone. Truly and deeply alone.

4

A Proposal

Belinda, Archie's widow—a pretty girl all of twenty years—accosted him in the courtyard the next morning.

"Sam Freeman, how dare you!"

He turned, only to have her fists hit him in the chest. He backed up, but she advanced, one arm clutching her child and the other swinging.

"Belinda, calm yourself." He didn't try and stop her but raised a hand to intercept the blows. There were tears in her eyes, but a look of rage in them.

"How dare you visit my husband's grave after what you've done?"

"What have I done to offend you?" Her blows were getting weaker, the tears stronger.

"You took my husband from me." Strands of dark brown hair fluttered in her face, then caught in the tracks on her cheeks. "He's dead because of you."

The accusation cut him to the core. Extreme sadness welled up inside him, sadness he thought he had left behind yesterday at the grave.

He caught her hand and held it. She cried out, trying to wrench it away. The baby was crying in her arms, screaming with fear.

"Belinda," he said, catching her up in his arms. She struggled, but then her struggles turned to sobs of pain, anger, and despair.

"What am I to do?" she cried through the tears.

Sam shut his eyes and held them both. What could he say to her? Could he ease her pain any more than his own?

He opened his mouth, dry at the lack of words. Sam licked his lips. "I don't know. I don't know what to do." He whispered the words, looking to the gray, cold sky.

It was unforgiving, just like life. A marriage ended, a future destroyed. A father taken to the grave.

It was his fate too, however he tried to fight it.

The cries of the baby died away as his mother calmed. She was warm.

Then, without warning, she pulled away. "Don't ever go to his grave again." Her bottom lip trembled. "He deserved better." She pulled the ragged blanket around her child, whispering in his ear to calm him.

"Belinda, there isn't anything I can say to help you feel any better." Sam stared into those red-streaked eyes, so full of fight and steel. He hadn't remembered that about her. He had always seen her as a soft, silly little thing, always giggling and unserious. "I miss Archie too."

She sniffed and raised her head. "He was a far better man than you are." A wave of emotion passed over her face again, and he thought she might cry. "I wish he'd never brought us to this forsaken place."

The baby cried out again, his eyes wide. Belinda leaned down and shushed him, rocking him from side to side.

He looked so much like Archie—his nose, his eyes. Sam stared into his little face, wondering how it came to be like that.

The truth is he could have done something for Archie long before. He was asked, but refused. Now, a child was fatherless.

Who was going to take care of him? His mother would care for him, of course, but what about her?

Who would provide food for her? A place over their heads? Clothes to wear?

He noticed that hers were in rough shape, a collection of worn clothes that were approaching rags. His own were only slightly better.

And the blanket she wrapped her child in was used and in tatters, held together only by the wrapping.

"Can I help you in any way?" Sam cringed at the words, how they came out.

Her eyes narrowed at him. "I've told you how you can help me. And make sure no one else gets killed." She spun on her heel and walked off, leaving him to ponder the conversation all the way to the workshop.

He stopped outside, looking back over the courtyard. Just a wall and a gate, now damaged and weakened by the fire. There was no wood to fix it, of any note, and the braces were left nailed to it.

All they had to do was break through that wall and storm across the courtyard. They could be in and through before they had a chance to secure the Keep.

There were so little defenses ready inside the castle that he was afraid any breach would end them.

Bill's shack was just there, across the way, and the plans he had proposed were still sound.

A twinge of guilt took him at not doing more sooner.

"Sam, is that you?" Ned asked from inside the workshop.

"It's me." He had his hand on the flap of the entrance but only slightly parted. Would Bill be willing?

That was a problem for another day. He only had a few hours until the appointed meeting time, if that, and a lot of work to get done.

The others were hard at work, almost exclusively making arrows. The stock of wood was getting lower every day, with no way to replenish it.

Sam went over to them, running his hand along the rough-cut timber. Most of it was seasoned, dry enough to work without much movement after they had moved all the wood that was most ready to be used before the attack.

He breathed in the deep smell of it, letting the oak, ash, and cherry push away his fears and failures.

The others made some small talk, but left him alone. Sam joined them, helping to make arrows, until the flap ruffled and Mathew appeared.

"Sam?" he asked, looking in with a question in his eyes.

Sam was putting away his tools and wrapping up the chisels. "I'm ready." He wiped the dust from his hands and joined Mathew at the door.

"Where are you going?" Trent asked, a touch of concern in his voice.

"I'll be back soon. I'll see you at lunch." Sam slipped out and let the flap fall down behind him.

"You weren't going to tell them?" The gravel crunched underfoot.

"No. I don't want to be there as is." Sam frowned, pulling his cloak tighter around him. Cold days had come in force. Even the warm sun on his skin couldn't keep him warm. "Let's get this over with."

Mathew was quiet the rest of the way, and Sam didn't feel much like talking. There was a storm brewing inside him, a collection of troubles in his mind.

He reached forward in time, thinking of what could happen. The walls were large, but not too long. With the men they had now it wouldn't be hard to keep them manned to repel an attack.

But each loss would be felt more and more. Day by day, their strength would lessen. Attack by attack, they would crumble.

Or were the Belmarch planning something else? He didn't know, but he did know the last attack cost them dearly. They had lost more men than the defenders.

They could be licking their wounds, letting their injured heal, all to prepare for another rush.

They were at the Keep now, the doors opened and shut behind them. Sam felt the thunder rise to a peak in front of the Overseer's door.

He took a deep breath.

Mathew was looking—or studying—the door. Sam couldn't tell which. His fingers twitched and trembled.

Sam put a hand on his shoulder and patted it. "Go on."

"I'm not so sure about this anymore. Maybe we'll get Verith to meet him instead." There were visible drops of sweat on his brow.

Instead of responding, Sam reached out a fist and knocked.

Mathew's eyes opened in surprise, and his jaw dropped. Sam gave him a shrug as they heard the Overseer respond.

"Come."

"Go on," Sam said, giving him a little push. Mathew reached out a trembling hand to the door and opened it.

"Mathew?" The Overseer put down a sheaf of paper, then, seeing Sam, opened a drawer in his desk and dropped it inside. "And... you."

Sam's heart dropped. He shouldn't have come. He knew that now, but the young man in front of him looked so pitiable,

"Overseer." Sam nodded respectfully and stood behind Mathew.

The Overseer's hard gaze lingered on Sam, then slipped to Mathew. The room smelled of tallow from the one candle in the corner and of must. It was unlit now, but Sam suspected it got its fair share of use, judging from how melted it was.

"Overseer Rhys," Mathew stammered, then remembering his place, saluted.

The silence drifted from long to uncomfortable.

"I imagine you had a reason for coming to see me?" The Overseer stared down from his seat.

Mathew's mouth worked. No sound came out. The Overseer tapped his fingers against the desk.

"Get on with it, then. Is there word from the wall?"

"No, Overseer. It... is another matter."

"And what of it?" The Overseer's tone was flustering Mathew, making him even more nervous than he was.

Sam watched on. He had a strange fascination with the whole scene. The young guard, the foppish leader. That this was the best they had to offer made him feel as if they had no chance at all.

He could offer a word of encouragement, give him something to hold onto. However, he knew that might make it worse from the way the Overseer had seen and dismissed him.

Instead, he opted for the least intrusive interjection, merely coughing quietly.

The Overseer's eyes snapped to him, and he gave him a gentle smile. Mathew straightened, a good sign.

"We need a leader, someone to oversee the daily defenses of the castle." The words spilled out of him, rushing all at once and almost joined together.

"Hold on, what do you mean?" The Overseer broke eye contact with Sam, turning his attention back to the guard. "This isn't a message?"

"No."

"Then what are you doing here? I have more important things to attend to."

Mathew hazarded a glance at Sam, who gave him a nod and a look of encouragement that he didn't feel himself.

The boy wasn't ready for this. The Overseer had always preferred to keep to himself and stay in his quarters while they worked on the castle. He would come out from time to time to bark orders and check on things, but he had never been the kind to train and encourage.

It was no surprise he was reacting this way. Sam should have known and anticipated it, told Mathew to expect it ahead of time. He felt shame.

Another list of things he should have done. A growing list, remembering Belinda and her words.

Mathew swallowed, shrinking back from the desk. His feet quivered, as if they were ready to run to the door.

He wasn't sure what to do. Sam wasn't sure either.

"Overseer..." Mathew swallowed, trying to gather his courage. Sam looked on with sadness.

If the man wasn't brave enough to make his case, how could he ever be expected to lead the other guards?

He was young. Too young to be caught up in all of this. Someone else needed to do it.

Looking over the Overseer, a soft man despite the lost weight that had slimmed him down, Sam knew he couldn't do it either. When Yand had died, they had lost more than a good fighter.

"I must entreat you in this matter," Mathew said. In the distance, a child cried, muted by the thick keep walls. "We must have someone to train the men. Someone who can lead them, if need be, in battle."

Sam half-expected the Overseer to start shouting, but what he did next surprised him. He sagged back into his chair, deflating.

"And what would you have me do? Pick up spear and sword? No, I think not."

"No, not have you do that."

"Then what?"

"I ask that you appoint a man for the task." At this, the Overseer rubbed his temples. There was already a man in the castle that was designated to lead, but that man had been shut away out of sight.

Go on, ask him. Sam willed Mathew to do what he came for.

"Will you do this? The men are crying out for it."

"And you are not the first to approach me on the matter. Out with it, ask your question."

Mathew took a deep breath, then spoke. "Put Sam Freeman in charge."

5

DISAGREEMENT

Sam's mouth dropped in surprise. He quickly shut it before the Overseer looked at him.

What was he thinking? This isn't what we agreed.

"Sam Freeman?" The Overseer looked at him now, his own eyes opened slightly in surprise.

"No," Sam said, meeting his gaze. "I can't do it."

"Well, we are in agreement. For once."

"Overseer, he's the only one with the leadership to do it. You've seen him fight. You know what he can do. He trained Trent to fight."

"Is this true?"

Bill. It had to be him. Would Trent reveal his night training to anyone? Sam didn't think so.

"Mathew has the wrong idea," Sam said. "He would be a good choice to lead, and you should make him the head guard."

"We all know that isn't right," Mathew said, hands clenched into fists. It didn't stop the quivering of them.

Sam felt sick. For all the same reasons he knew Mathew wasn't right, he had still said it. His eyes dropped to the floor.

Silence seeped into the room. Sam could feel his own breath in his chest, the hard stones of the floor beneath his feet.

His mind wandered back to the past, to all the other places he wished he'd rather not be. A cold battlefield frozen in the winter. A hot graveyard still reeking of blood under the unforgiving sun.

He didn't hate the Overseer, but he didn't like him either. The man was weak in some respects and hard in others. The wrong things.

But he wasn't stupid, and he knew how to handle himself in situations like these. Sam suspected that might be one of the reasons he was put in charge, despite not having any experience building castles before.

Not that many did. There weren't many castles in Chathem, but plenty of watchtowers.

He doubted that anyone had the experience to build one, which might have been why it had taken longer than expected.

Cloth shifted, rubbing against itself as the Overseer leaned back in his chair. It creaked, protesting the injustice, but stopped.

"We're going to die if we don't know what to do," Mathew said, stealing Sam away from his thoughts. "Would you ask the Duke?"

"I make no promises to you. Particularly this impudent request." The Overseer once again cast his gaze over Sam. It slid off him like oil on water.

"Mathew, he's right. I'm not the right man to lead anything," Sam said. What he wanted was a different life, to build.

"You took a risk, like all of us." The Overseer clasped his hands together. "Striking deep into almost the very heart of the enemy. You knew this day would come."

He was talking to Sam, who wisely held his tongue.

"I wonder why. Would you like to enlighten us?"

"Money," Sam said. "Like the other men here." The Overseer let out a bark of a laugh, incredulous.

"Is that why you came, Mathew? For the money?" He turned his attention to the guard.

"For the chance to advance, Overseer." Mathew hung his head. "And the money."

"Which you, no doubt, have realized is now contingent on our survival. Yes, money can be a great motivator. I'm not sure it is the motivation, though, for all." The Overseer waved his hand. "I will consider your request. Again, I make no promises."

Mathew was going to get out of it without getting in trouble, of that Sam was glad, but he couldn't let this rest.

"I beg you not to consider it." Sam stepped forward, taken by a mood. What was he to lead anything?

"That will be enough from you," the Overseer snapped. He picked up a quill, preparing to dip it into his ink. "You have had your say."

Sam didn't think that he had, and leaned forward, putting his hands on the desk. The way the man spoke to him, like he was filth, dirt on his shoes, angered him.

A word, a little phrase spoken, could end this for him. Sam knew it and locked eyes with the Overseer.

They were cool, calculating. Gone was the bubbling old fool hidden in the folds of fat. There was something else in there.

Something dangerous.

I can end any chance now. He never liked me. He hates me.

"If you have something to say to me, say it." The Overseer spoke in a whisper, weight behind his words.

He had something to say.

"Good afternoon, Overseer." Sam let go of the desk, feeling the blood rush back to his fingers, and stepped back.

He turned and walked out of the room. Mathew hastily bid his farewell, maintaining his decorum, and followed.

He caught up to Sam in the hallway, grabbing his arm.

"Sam, I—"

"That isn't what we discussed." Sam spun around, advancing on the man, who shrunk back.

"There is no one else." There was pain in Mathew's eyes. "I'm sorry."

"There are plenty of men."

"Not in this castle. You have to understand what we're up against. It isn't a game."

"No," Sam growled, "it isn't." He didn't know why he was dumb enough not to see it before. This was always Mathew's plan.

"What chance do we have without you?" Mathew looked in his eyes, searching for something.

Sam turned without answering him and walked away.

He was a mixture of emotions. Anger, fear, loathing. Most of it was directed at himself. The rest was directed toward Mathew.

"I'll tell you what chance you have. None. Even with me, you have no chance." Sam waved his hand. "Look around you. Do you see anyone coming to help us? Do you see an army marching to the rescue?"

He couldn't see, but Mathew shrank back as if hit.

"If you want my help, then I can give you some advice. Make your peace, and prepare for death. That's what you'll get in this place. That's what you'll get with me."

Before Mathew could answer Sam spun on his heel and took off as fast as he could. His feet clattered on the stone floor, a soft sound in the long hallway. He didn't hear Mathew try and come after him.

Sam left the Keep, fleeing to the north wall and away from as many as he could. It was more peaceful up here, to the tower he climbed, and in little fear of attack.

The Golden River churned below him, the river running over the rocks at the base of the wall.

Sam leaned against the wall, letting the cold wind bite through his coat. The first snowflake of the year drifted down from the white, puffy clouds high in the sky.

His breath came out in clouds, streaming behind him in the wind as it was carried away. Where had all the time gone?

It had seemed like summer would never end a few months ago, and now it was snatched away. Sam closed his eyes and listened to the world.

The river talked above his heartbeat, strong and steady and shivering along the rocks. Birds called up above him, latecomers as they traveled south.

Behind him the sounds of the castle were muted, a thick wall in between him and the others.

They were out of the frying pan now, and smack dab in the middle of the fire. He opened his eyes, hoping for a moment they would reveal the Chathem army just out of sight.

Instead, he was given the sight of an empty and cold river. Never-ending, barren, desolate. No hope of survival, no plan for saving.

He looked south. A few days' journey that direction and they would be at the port city of Jareth. Bale would be a few more days inland, and then a message delivered.

So how, exactly, were they going to get that message delivered?

He had been on boats before, but was in no way a riv-er-man. A crossing here and there. That was the extent of his experience.

Would it be possible to resupply the castle from the water? Sam squinted, trying to see beneath the surface of the river.

Those who had grown up on the water, or made their livelihoods on it, might be able to make sense of how the water moved around the base of the castle, but to Sam it was impossible.

The water came up to the bank of rock, hit it and swirled around, then continued on to wherever it went. Nothing stopped it, and it kept going.

The bell rang out in the courtyard. Changing of the guard.

Sam sighed and slipped down the steps to the courtyard below. It was his turn—another few hours of standing and waiting, shivering on the battlements and staring at an enemy that wanted to destroy them.

He went to the courtyard outside the barracks, received his bow and allotment of arrows, managing to avoid Mathew.

He followed the others up the steps to the wall, taking his place on the south wall to the west of the gate.

"Any change?" Sam asked, approaching Stave, who he was charged with taking over from.

"Nothing." Stave spit over the edge. "Other than this forsaken cold."

They exchanged words, and Sam bid him a good night. Stave tipped his hat to him and left.

He was a mason, but wasn't as chilly toward him as he used to be. Sam noticed this and noted it for later.

Perhaps Bill was telling them to lay off him, or maybe something else was going on. He wouldn't be surprised if it was a ploy to get him to agree to...

Rebellion. Sam shivered. How could he even consider it?

But they were in desperate times, and men in these kinds of situations did desperate things.

What had driven Bill to it? Was it something in his past, a proclivity to it?

Something moved in the distance. A man appeared at the edge of the Belmarch camp and stopped. The figure moved around, then went back inside.

A few more streamed out of the camp. They, too, had their change of guard. They went into the forest, hidden from the prying eyes of the defenders, and dispersed to wherever they had set their watches.

Sam tried to follow them, hand tightening on his unstrung bow. He thought they might turn to the castle, launch an attack.

But they didn't. A few minutes later, men emerged, probably the relieved, and went into the camp.

Their fire burned where the old Square had been, bright and cheery with happy billows of smoke.

The nerve they had to do it. Sam had spent a few happy nights there, filled with food, laughter, and decent ale that slaked the thirst after a long day of work.

It was a different time, one he had hoped would last forever, but one he knew must end. He had hoped it would be after the completion of the castle. Sam would have stayed, been a resident of the new town to be built within its walls, safely nestled behind the gray stone.

Instead, they were trapped here. He leaned against the hard stone, watching the forest for any sign of movement.

It was quiet and still. The bare trees had gained a dusting of snow, but it had stopped.

The cold was draining his feet of heat, his shoes long ago in need of repair. He would have to see if he could get a few rags to wrap around his feet to keep them warm, but until he did, he had to resort to lifting first one, then the other, after he couldn't bear the chill anymore.

The rest of the watch passed with little to note. Only that dull monotony he had grown so accustomed to.

He hated it. Always had. Better to be dressing lumber than sit doing nothing all day.

It was a relief when the dinner bell rang, and Kerien came to relieve him about a half-hour later.

"Evening," Sam said, slapping his arms to regain some heat.

"Mmm," Kerien grunted.

"Dinner not good?"

"No. You'll see." Kerien's eyes narrowed as he looked to the enemy camp. "Is that...?"

"Best not to think about it too much." Sam's mouth was watering. "They're doing it on purpose."

Kerien groaned. "What I'd give for a bite of that."

The Belmarch had killed a deer and were roasting it on a spit over the fire. Every so often, a flare from the fire would raise up as a dripping caught fire and was consumed.

"I think they want to kill us, but they're willing to take their time."

"Gruel, again. And cold."

Sam frowned but hiked up his bow and took up his arrows. "Good watch."

Kerien stared, and Sam left him.

They were going to wait them out, let them all starve to death. As Sam's cold feet squished the thin layer of snow, he knew he couldn't let that happen.

The problem was, what was he to do about it?

What good would it have done, anyway?

He strode across the cold floor, giving greetings to those who had the heart to look up at him and respond back.

Their bowls and dishes were filled with more of the same. Sam grimaced. He wasn't looking forward to this.

"Good evening, Martha," he said, producing his bowl from beneath his tattered coat. "Mutton stew tonight?"

She narrowed her eyes at him and wagged the spoon in his direction. "None of your jokes tonight, Sam. I don't have the heart to hear it."

"What's wrong?" He didn't mean to offend her.

"It's Mary. I don't know what's wrong with her, but the stubborn girl refuses to work." She reached into the pot with the spoon, wiggled it around a little, then scooped out a clump. It clung to the pot, fighting as if it wanted to stay, but then came off with a slop.

Into his proffered bowl it went. She banged a few times to get it to release. "I see," he said sympathetically. "Anything wrong with her?"

"You know what's wrong with her. Heartbroken." Her normally hard eyes turned soft and glistened in the dim light. He sniffed at his bowl. It smelled like water and wheat. Unsurprisingly, that was what it was.

He thought.

"Her, among others." His first thought was of Belinda. Alone, afraid, with a young son to take care of and no father to help. His heart tweaked, and shame rose inside. "It has come to hard times."

"But we expected hard times, didn't we?" She sighed and leaned over her bowl. "Coming up here. Doing what we did. My poor Davy wanted me to stay away, but I told him that by his side was where I'd pledged to be, and by his side, I'd stay."

"An admirable quality."

"Not everyone agreed with me. They'll be wishing they were here now."

"I doubt that very much." Not all the families had come. Some stayed with family and friends elsewhere, unaccustomed or unwilling to pull up their roots. Not until the castle and walls were complete and a full garrison stationed, at least.

Sam couldn't blame them, and often felt bad for the men who barely saw their families. He wondered what they thought now and looked down the line of tables.

There was Eric, a stonemason with a young wife and no children. His wife had stayed behind with her mother. Sam had overheard her say as much.

And there were others. Eric seemed to be doing fine, other than looking skinnier than he used to be.

"What about you, Sam? Leave a sweetheart behind?" Martha twirled her spoon around. There was no one in line behind him to hold up.

"No one." His meal was getting cold. He knew he should go sit down and eat. It was better lukewarm.

"I'm sorry to hear that." She sounded it too, genuine. He had often wondered how life would have turned out if he had stayed.

Would he be promised out to someone by now? Living in the countryside with babies? His former home was a peaceful place now, by all accounts, the old wars calm and settled, and general camaraderie with neighbors.

Since they had won their freedom, at least, from the assessor. But that had been a long time ago now.

"What will you do after this?" Martha asked, bringing him back from his thoughts.

"I hadn't thought about it." He wondered if there would be an after.

6

STORM IN THE KEEP

The door slammed shut behind him. Blessedly, it stopped the wind from cutting through his cloak. Sam rubbed feeling back into his arms.

The Keep wasn't warm, but it wasn't as cold as outside.

The great hall had been returned to its former status, or rather, what it would be when complete. Tables ran down both sides, rough timbers that had been repurposed from their original intended use within the Keep itself.

Men and women sat at them, eating out of bowls and drinking from cups of wood.

It was the body heat of everyone inside that kept away the worst of the cold. The fireplace was cold and bare.

How he wished it were filled with logs cracking orange and red, sending their smoke into the room and up the chimney. Instead, it was wet and dead.

At the far end Martha was serving food. She had become a de facto leader of the women, keeping them busy and directing their efforts.

Once plump and rounded, she had slimmed down. Her straight, black hair accentuated the change, making her face seem thin and drawn.

What must I look like?

Sam stroked his beard, now three inches long. It had kept out the worst of the cold. His hair hung shabby and long. He hadn't had the time or the desire to cut it.

"What will you do?"

"My family is from down south, in Bevonshire." The cook-fire was out now, banked down to preserve every bit of wood and fuel. She had wrinkles at the corners of her eyes, just beginning to show. "I think I'll go back."

Sam wondered if he should ask about her husband, lost to the sickness that took so many. He had wondered why she had stayed here. But he thought better of it.

"What's it like?" He scooped up his meal. Here was as good as any.

"I'll join you. You were one of the last." She turned her head back to one of the younger girls. "Nancy, watch the food."

They sat down at the table. "It's a peaceful place. More sheep than people." Martha slipped behind the table and sat gracefully.

"It sounds nice."

"Except when you have to shear them. The smell." She wrinkled her nose up. "Worse than rotted food if you don't clean them well enough. Or it rains." She tilted her head off to the side. "Nothing like the smell of damp sheep." A faint smile played over her lips.

Sam looked away, painfully aware that he had been staring at them. "I can't say I've smelled it. Or that I've seen many."

"You haven't seen sheep?" Martha laughed. It was strange—there had been so little laughter around here. "Well, that is unbelievable."

"Is it?"

"What about you? What reminds you of home?"

Home. That was something he wasn't sure what to call. He took a bite of his food. It was bland but edible. It stuck to the roof of his mouth.

"You're avoiding the question."

"Mmm-hmm." He pointed to his mouth, trying to ignore her eyes, filled with a touch of mirth and a dollop of annoyance. "Not trying. Just hungry. The forest. That reminds me of home."

"Is that what drew you to working wood?"

"I hadn't thought about that before. I liked walking through it, cool in the summer when the sun was so harsh in the pen. The way the leaves crunch under my feet and tickle my toes." The memory of it made the hall disappear for a moment.

He was back on the path now, walking beside the brook as it bubbled and worked its way down the hill. The smell of the leaves was thick, the summer raging, but it was cool.

Is that where I want to be?

"I'm not sure what my home will be, or when I'll get there." Her eyes seemed to ache.

Was that for him? Or something else? "Thank you for the meal, for leading the other women." He finished the meager portion left. "I should go. We have a lot of work to do." True enough, for now, but what would he do when they had no supplies, when they had no work to occupy themselves?

It nagged at him, it burrowed into his brain and refused to go away. They would need more food if they were to last. They would need more wood if they were to build.

But they still had plenty of rock. It was just Bill who he needed now. Command him, and he had the masons.

Martha's face fell. "I will see you at dinner."

Sam felt hot all of a sudden, unaware of what he had said. She stood up and rushed off back to the other girls, starting to give directions before she got there.

There was a creeping feeling on his back, but Sam pushed it off to the side. He did have a lot of work to do.

How he would handle it all, he wasn't sure.

***

The world was a groggy haze. Sunlight snuck in at the top of his room, casting a harsh glare upon everything.

Evan groaned. His head was pounding, and he felt sick to his stomach. He opened his eyes, cracked and dry.

Next to his head was a pile of vomit. It smelled horrible, so he turned away. The residue of it cracked at the corners of his mouth.

What time it was, he did not know, nor did he care. He wanted to go back to sleep, but the drink had worn off. He wasn't sure what kind of dreams would haunt him.

They still did, despite the wine. His father standing over him, bringing down his sword in retribution, his eyes burning like fire as it consumed him.

Evan squeezed his eyes shut again, trying to banish the thought. Overseer Rhys hadn't come to see him yet—it must be before noon.

Unless he had given up.

He tried to get out of bed, shoving off the covers. His head swam as he sat up, and he almost fell back again.

What am I doing? Back to my old ways.

He just needed a pack of pigs, and everything would be complete.

The ground was cold, the bare stone sapping the warmth from his feet. He was still in his clothes, not bothering to change apparently. He didn't remember much from last night after the fifth or sixth glass of wine.

Had he really drunk that much?

The goblet was on the table, knocked over. He shuffled over to it, making sure to go slow so that he wouldn't fall over.

The bottle was empty. The one next to it too.

There was a cask in the cellar left. Three or four, he couldn't remember. He didn't pay much attention to the numbers when Rhys droned on.

"Attention to the management of your lands is hardly exciting," his father had said one afternoon when he had drifted off to sleep. *"Those who neglect it are foolish."*

He had been only nine or ten summers old then, but he remembered it like it was yesterday.

His mouth ached for a drink. It felt dry, like cotton, and he wished for something to slake the memory. To wash it all away.

It would be washed away, one way or the other. His father would never take him back now, let alone his uncle. What a disgrace to the family.

The tree whose roots run deep? Not mine, he thought bitterly.

Where was that servant? Evan rang the bell and waited, but no one came. He rang it louder. They were supposed to be right there, waiting in case he needed something.

"Is there no discipline around here?" he growled. "Who's out there?"

There was no response. Head pounding, Evan tugged on his boots and stumbled to the door.

It wasn't quiet like it usually was. Every so often, there was a loud bang.

He wrenched open the door, scowling.

The corridor was empty, not a servant in sight.

"Where are they?" He stepped out into the hallway. "Hello?"

There were shouts, but from outside, and he couldn't make out what they were saying.

Some of his hangover receded, replaced with fear. *What was going on?*

He went back inside, hurrying to strap on his sword. His fingers were thick and slow, and he fumbled with the clasp. Finally, the metal ends clicked together, and it was around his waist.

He went back to the door, then stopped. He didn't want to go out there, to find out what was happening. He wanted a drink.

His eyes shifted to the right, to his study. There would certainly be more there. To his left was the exit, out into the courtyard.

He hadn't been out there in weeks. Every time he tried, he couldn't make it. It was as if there was a hand pushing on his chest, crushing him. Preventing him from going out.

A few steps, a few doors. That was all that he had to do.

Evan shook his head, fell against the door. Instead of taking that path, he went back to his study, fingers trembling as he opened the door.

He got inside and locked it, a great weight off his chest, but a wave of shame to replace it.

He should be out there. He should be with his people. But they weren't his, really—they were his father's.

The great seal of the Hornbloods loomed above him over his desk. He looked away. He couldn't bear it.

What was happening outside? It didn't sound like fighting, not exactly. He had heard that before, but it didn't sound pleasant either.

He could make out the ringing of something—sword on sword, he thought.

All the blood drained from his face. What if they were inside? That they had taken the outer walls?

Only the walls of the Keep would keep them out. Only a thin layer of rock was between his sworn enemy and himself.

And there was nothing he could do to stop it. His hand clutched at his sword, both a comfort and a reminder of what he should be doing.

His nose was running, and he wiped it with his sleeve. Pressure, there was so much pressure. He shrank down.

He felt pinned against the door. That hand, there it was again. His breath was short, his chest on fire.

Sweat was running down his forehead, despite the cold of the room. Clammy hands pulled at his collar.

His head still ached. He wished he was anywhere other than here. Agony filled his body, his mind, his soul.

Evan Hornblood collapsed to the floor, his sword ringing against the stone. He should draw it, charge outside, and face the Belmarch head-on.

He could go out in a blaze of glory, one man against a thousand, sword flashing in the sun like a blade of fire.

But he was here, cowering on the ground.

Yand wouldn't have said anything. He would have picked him up, dusted him off, and sent him to the training yards.

He would have beat him in combat training, not with the whip. Even now, he remembered those lessons—the forms, the exercises.

But here he was. Evan moaned and caught a glimpse of the tree again.

It was too large, too overpowering. Blast that carpenter who made it. He should have chucked it into the fire. His own pride had done him in.

He pulled himself to the bar and took out a bottle.

It was empty.

The next was empty too. Bottles flew as he flung them away, crashing and cracking, some shattering into a million pieces.

There wasn't a single drop of wine left.

Evan slunk to his knees. He was going to die in this room. Alone, and like a coward.

There were voices outside his room, rough voices shouting something he couldn't make out.

They are here!

Evan pulled himself to his desk and crawled under it. The door rattled and shook.

There, hiding beneath his desk, Evan felt the worst he had ever felt in his life.

Something cracked inside him. He wasn't going to die like this.

Pushing aside the pain, the shame, the cowardice, he rose to his feet and drew his sword.

"Come and take me if you can," he shouted, then strode to the door and unlocked it.

7

Hope Less

Evan braced himself, eyes bloodshot and heart pounding, as the invaders slammed open the door.

He gave a war cry and raised his sword.

Overseer Rhys raised his hands in defense. "Sire!"

Evan stopped himself before the blow landed, breathing hard. "Rhys, what... what's going on?"

"Someone heard sounds from your room. I had to come check." Still shaken, the Overseer rose from where he had crumpled down to avoid death.

"I called for the servants. I—where were they?"

"Apologies, my lord, I had them in the storeroom. The others were busy with practice."

He ran a hand through his hair, now giddy. "We aren't under attack?"

"No, your highness." Evan turned, looking down at the sword in his hand and the remains of the bottles around his room.

There was a strange feeling inside him. The longing for the wine, that escape, was still there.

But there was something bigger than it, something that overcame it. He laughed suddenly, and turned.

The servants behind Rhys looked at each other in concern. Evan clapped the Overseer on the back. "Apologies for the smell. It seems I got carried away. Give me some time to wash up and we can discuss matters."

Surprise was an understatement for the look that flashed across Rhys' face, but he covered it up quickly. "Certainly, we still need some time to finish the inventory. I will come by as soon as we are done."

The overpowering feeling of relief was still there when they left, and Evan couldn't stand still. He paced around his room, alternating between laughing and frowning.

He had been a coward, there was no use in lying to himself. He had taken the easy way out.

That was the Evan of yesterday, though. Now, he was a different man. The simple act of defiance, being prepared to die with a sword rather than cowering beneath a desk, was heady and filled him with giddiness.

For the first time in a long time, he had hope that things might change. And, as he looked up at his looming family crest, a glimmer of hope that he might be worthy of the name Hornblood.

***

A soft knock at the door reached him at his desk. "Come."

Overseer Rhys walked in, a bundle of scraps of paper and records under his arm. "Good afternoon, your highness."

"Come, come, sit down." Evan motioned to the open chair. Even though his head still ached from the hangover, the cold bath and clean clothes had done wonders for it. His bed was being washed now, a luxury he knew the others might not have.

The Overseer glanced at his hair, combed for the first time in weeks, and over his clothes, but he sat without comment.

"I haven't been the best Duke," Evan said, "and we might as well address that now."

"Your highness," the Overseer protested, but Evan cut him off.

"We'll move past it, no need for flowery words to try and cover it up. Once we're done here, I need to go inspect the guardhouse and the walls, see what state they're in. Father always said seeing the thing was far more important than hearing about it." Rhys had always included a report with his meetings.

His words caused a strange tightness around the Overseer's eyes and lips. "What is it? I'm certain you've done what you can, and I have no reservations about what you've told me."

"That isn't it." He took his time to answer. The Overseer was choosing his words carefully, and Evan leaned in when he finally said them. "It might be best to be out of sight. The men are... restless."

His heart dropped, and his voice caught in his throat. "You don't mean...?"

The Overseer nodded. "You're safer inside."

"I don't believe it."

"It's rumors, your highness, but these rumors tend to lead to... nasty results."

Evan shook his head. Then, anger rose up inside him. "They would dare overthrow their lawful ruler? I'll have their heads on pikes."

"Talk like that might not have the most soothing effect." The Overseer's face looked drawn and tight. "The rule of law is already on the edge of a knife. One push might be all it takes."

"Surely you exaggerate?" More than a hint of fear entered his voice. His father was right to send him here, to prove that he would fail.

Or had he sent him to redeem himself, to prove that he could handle a situation like this?

Either way, this ill news was too much to bear. The thirst came back, that precious liquid that would send him into oblivion. He would take a peasant's homebrew if he could get it.

"Perhaps I've misjudged the situation." The Overseer didn't look like he had any doubt of it, though. *Blasted politician.* "But a few more days of caution might be called for. You can rest and recover from your…" He paused, then found the word he was looking for. "Ordeal."

And that was that. The topic covered, the Overseer brought out his inventory and records and proceeded to drone through them.

Evan paid more attention this time, but he couldn't help but think about it, always clouding his thoughts like a thunderhead in summer a few miles off.

A looming threat, that might dissipate and blow to dust, or one that could take a sharp turn and be on you in an instant. One would be easy to bear, the other required good shelter.

So, what would he do if it were true?
***

The guards sweated and groaned as they trained, the tradesmen even more so.

Sam trudged by them, glad that his squad was not until after dinner.

"Sam, wait up." Mathew joined him, matching him stride for stride. He couldn't help but feel a hint of annoyance, and it must have shown on his face.

"Have you reconsidered?"

"There isn't anything to consider. Didn't you hear Overseer Rhys?" He seemed warm against the bitter cold. Sam remembered that feeling, being hot despite the cold.

He wondered if they should be doing it. Training was important, but it was taking energy. That, in turn, led them to hunger faster.

It would be a drain on their food. The training would need to be focused, and only what they needed, nothing more, to avoid waste.

Even now, he observed two men sparring and doing a terrible job of it. They circled each other, bashing one another with their swords. It would have been fine in a normal army, but here it was wasteful and unneeded. Every excess movement was a waste, from how they swung too much and lunged too far.

"I see you'd like a turn?"

Mathew stared at him, and Sam broke his gaze. *If he said anything...*

"Just watching." Mathew's face fell. "You should get back to training."

"There isn't much else to do, other than watch."

Little did he know. That was a blessing. "I must go." He bid Mathew farewell and strode off, letting him fall behind.

Bill was there, and Sam felt his eyes on his back.

Sam hurried into the workshop, eager to pick up his tools again. His work helped ease his mind, and the time passed quickly.

Dinner came faster than he realized, the peals of the bell ringing out. Everyone looked up as it started and relaxed when it was the simple call to dinner.

They put away tools and streamed out, but someone caught hold of his arm as he went.

It was Bill, motioning for him to keep quiet. Sam furrowed his brow, but he only nodded his head and slipped inside the workshop.

"I forgot something, you all go on ahead," Sam said, waving the others away. When they had gone, confused looks on their faces, he went back in.

Bill was at his workbench, touching his tools. "Hands off," Sam said, his voice gruff and lower than normal. His body had tensed up at the sight.

Bill stopped, then raised his hands with a smirk. "I mean no harm. Nor insult either."

After taking a deep breath, Sam remembered his manners. He shouldn't have done that. "What is it you want to talk about?"

"I think you know."

"I grow tired of these men."

"I presume you expect me to have changed my mind?"

"You know the rumors just as well as I do."

Sam folded his hands across his chest and leaned back against the wooden support of the workshop. A faint hint of smoke was in the air. He wondered if it was from the meal or if it was from the Belmarch camp.

Sometimes it seemed like they did it to torment them, creating huge bonfires that you could almost imagine feeling from the top of the wall.

It was torture, but didn't drive the men to do what the Duke was doing.

"I haven't heard the latest. Enlighten me."

Bill ran a finger along a board, picking up some sawdust. He crushed it between his finger and thumb, rubbing it around. "Life has become... too much to bear for the Duke. He's draining the wine faster than if it had holes in the cask."

It was the same rumor he had heard. Late nights, sleeping through the day. "That doesn't give anyone the right to kill him."

"Kill?" Bill's eyes opened in feigned surprise, and he held up his hands. "Who said anything about killing?"

Sam narrowed his eyes by reflex.

"I never said I wanted to kill the Duke. He needs to be set aside though. He isn't fit to lead."

Sam almost defended the Duke but wasn't sure where to start.

"Ah, I see it in your eyes. You agree but don't want to admit it."

"Why haven't you done it by yourself?"

"I've thought about it, but you and I know the rest of the men aren't in my grip the way the masons are. And I couldn't convince all of them on my own, even if I wanted to."

"You want someone else to do your dirty work, so that your hands stay clean."

"Not necessarily, although I have thought of it." Bill shrugged. "I want to get out of here alive, Sam. Both you and I know it won't happen unless we have someone who can lead and inspire the men."

He was stroking his ego to try and get him to do what he wanted. Sam saw through it, but his voice seemed so sincere. "You've mastered lying."

"We need to get help, and no one else seems to want to take charge," Bill said. "If we do that first, if we can work together to find a way to get aid, would that satisfy you?"

"No, it wouldn't. He's the Duke, the future ruler of this castle."

"He's a drunken little boy who is going to get all of us killed," Bill hissed. "What good will he do ruling over a grave?"

"Then you go to him. You convince him to abdicate and leave the power to you." Bill started, and Sam pressed the attack. "You never thought of that, have you? Always quick to anger and never to the simple solution."

"He won't do it. I know men. They don't give up power willingly."

"You don't know that. The Duke may not want to be here. He may be more than glad to get out of the way for you to lead."

"You're trying to distract me, to keep me confused." Bill shook his head. "I won't have it, not this time."

"No one is coming to save us. Face the truth, Bill."

"Since when did Sam Freeman become so hopeless?" The wind lifted the flap of the workshop and blew sawdust up, scattering chips and curls of wood.

Had he given up hope? He caught a glimpse of the spear, its broken handle shattered still, and wondered.

It seemed to him that there was no choice. They were too few and too ill-trained to try and counterattack.

Unless...

"You haven't answered my question. Will you reconsider if we can get help?"

"No." Bill started to walk out. "What did you have in mind?"

Bill shook his head. "We'll talk another time."

The flap swung back and forth when he left, until it finally came to a stop. Sam pulled his coat tighter. The worst of winter hadn't even come yet.

He closed his eyes and leaned against his workbench. A million thoughts raced through his mind, all competing for attention.

Bill was right about one thing. If they didn't get someone to lead them soon, they might not survive another night.

Every time he tried to avoid it, he kept coming back to the same conclusion.

There was only one man with fighting experience in the castle. One man who had led before and could lead again.

He had to do something.

There, in the dark of the workshop he used to create, Sam decided.

8

HANDED DOWN FROM ONE TO ANOTHER

Evan paced his room. The walls felt like they were closing in on him. It had been so long since he had seen the sun that he wasn't sure what it looked like anymore.

Even though the chill of winter was in the air, leaking through the stone and cracks in the walls, he still thought it was stuffy inside.

Ever present, his desire for drink ate at him. Less than a hundred feet below him, the remaining three casks of wine were stored below in the cellar.

His mouth watered at the thought, the distraction that would take him away from this room, away from his troubles.

A candle flickered by his bedside, giving off the smell of tallow in its small flame. It seemed like it would go out at any moment, the candle down to a stub. He had asked for a new one, but the Overseer had refused.

He refused him! He was no Duke in this place, not anymore.

The shadow of his father haunted him, stroked behind him, ever out of sight. He thought he could see him sometimes, at the corner of his eye, but when he turned his head, nothing was there.

The days had become a blur. One day stretched into the next. Only the small amount of light coming through his study window let him know that time was moving on. For all he knew, they weren't progressing through time at all.

His stomach rumbled. It must be getting close to dinner, but he balked at the thought of eating. The meat was all gone, eaten days ago, and they were down to the dredges of vegetables and grains stored in the cellar.

A knock sounded on his door. He bade them enter.

A servant entered and set down his plate. Evan felt his mouth water even as he saw what was on it. A bland porridge of water-soaked oats and wheat. Uncooked, hard, barely softened by the water they kept it in overnight. The servant departed, and he sat down to eat.

He longed for the days of his youth now, the great hunting parties that brought back fresh venison and game to a table loaded with food of every kind. The kitchens of the Arch Duke were always staffed by the best cooks, who might even be able to make this palatable, given enough time.

But he was too hungry to reject it and ate. There was a hint of something, and he dug around in the bowl. It looked like, among the mush, there were spots of brown. He looked closer and tasted one. Mushroom. It gave the meal a bit of earthy flavor, welcome after such a bland time. *Where had they found them?*

It brought him back to the days of his youth, to the harvest festivals in the Hornwood. His mouth watered with the thought of those mushrooms—some as big as a man's head—that popped up in the dark places of the forest where men feared to tread, then baked like pies in the ovens of the palace.

Even then, he had felt the sting of loneliness, watching the other boys and girls at play on the palace grounds. He remembered slipping out one night to try and join them, thinking he was clever in slipping his guard.

They had known it was him, even in the dark. None of the other children would play with him. They called him "Your Grace" and bowed and scraped, then fled as soon as they could.

What would it have been like to have a normal childhood, to laugh and play and not have a care in the world? They didn't have to carry the weight of a dukedom on their shoulders. They didn't know what it was like to bear the future of his people on his back.

It was crushing. Even now, he itched for a good glass of icy ale, a thick, foamy head on it that clung to his lips and tickled his nose. He sighed, imagining the thick, hoppy smell of his favorite brew from down in the valley.

What am I thinking? He knew he was restless, cooped up like a dog in a kennel. He wanted to be outside, to see the sunlight again, and considered the Overseer's words.

What if it wasn't the men who wanted to overthrow him, but Rhys himself? What better way to seize power than to feed him a stream of lies designed to keep him afraid?

He longed for Yand and his counsel, once more feeling his absence keenly. What would he have said? What would he have advised?

Wallowing in self-pity in his room would not have been his words, let alone his counsel. Evan pushed the empty plate away, still hungry.

What would father do? The man seemed as hard as iron but would bend if he needed to. Had he ever faced a situation like this? Evan doubted it.

He saw again the image of himself on horseback, leading a charge out of the gate and smashing the enemy ranks to pieces. His sword flashed in the glorious sunlight, red with the blood of the invaders.

He gnawed on his lip and wondered, thinking of a way to get out of this situation. He thought until the sun was gone and his room was as dim as a cave.

Even when everything was black, he kept thinking. Long into the night, until his eyelids were too heavy to keep open anymore.

He still didn't know what to do.

***

"I'll do it."

Mathew jumped, surprised at the sound of his voice, then turned. "What will you do?"

Sam grimaced. "I'll train the men," he said through gritted teeth. The only other option would be to have them die or spoiled by poor instruction.

"That's great news." A smile spread across Mathew's face.

"There's a catch." Sam held up a finger. "You'll have to convince the Overseer yourself. I'm not going to go groveling to him about it."

"I wouldn't dream of it." Mathew looked around. "Here, we're starting earlier tomorrow. What can you teach us?"

"What are you doing?"

Mathew was rummaging around the barracks now, looking in chests and the solitary cupboard that sat in the corner.

"I'm looking for—here it is."

He turned and held out a stick, pulled from behind the cupboard.

"What are you going to do with a practice sword?" Sam felt his eyebrows arch on their own accord.

"Not just any practice sword. This was Captain Yand's practice sword." Mathew held it out. "You should take it. I'll find a way to convince the Overseer that it's the right decision."

It lay there, smoothed from years of use, shining in the dingy barracks. Someone had polished it recently, but it couldn't hide the dents and scratches of what must have been a thousand sparring sessions.

He remembered it well, how Yand had wielded it like an expert.

"It should not come to me."

"You need to take it." Mathew thrust it at him again. "No one else deserves it."

"I don't deserve it."

"We know what you did. Some of us saw what you did on the walls. You took down that giant."

"It is not for me." Sam pushed it away.

"You gave us hope." Mathew's eyes were glistening, and his words moved Sam.

What would it mean? To take up the sword of a dead man? Would he fall under its owner's fate? Would he too be destined to die in this place? A whisper from the door broke him out of the questions.

"I don't deserve this." Sam put his hand around the hilt and closed it on the cool wood. Even this had taken winter upon it. "But I will take it. I will do my best."

There is no going back now.

"Thank you." Mathew turned. "I was afraid it would fall upon me."

A weight had descended on Sam, pressing on his shoulders. *Was this what Mathew felt?*

He was too young. They all were, even the old like Ned.

"Before nightfall, we will assemble in the yard." They had taken to calling it that—the section of the courtyard reserved for practice that the children played on when it was vacant.

It was hard-packed earth now, stamped by the feet of many men over many days. Sam considered the training sword and felt a twinge of annoyance and a hint of... what was it?

Hatred.

Duke Hornblood should be taking this sword. Duke Hornblood should be out here every day.

He knew what Bill felt, but he knew it wasn't right. He was the rightful ruler of the castle, not Sam.

Why then did he refuse to rule? It made him afraid that he was starting to see the sense in what Bill had to say.

"I will meet you then." Sam left him.

The wind grabbed at his cloak, and Sam had to hold onto it as he left the barracks. His teeth started chattering a second later. The sky was gray. It would be colder when the sun went down. *A perfect time to attack.*

If the conditions were right. So far, they didn't seem to be. Or the Belmarch were content to let them starve. Every day, he expected another attack. Every day, it was the same. The watchers on the walls would grow complacent. They would expect each night to be quiet.

Were they lulling us into complacency, just to have them strike? It was so confusing. Webs within webs of plans, and every one could be a false assumption that made your enemy stronger than he really was.

It was going to take all he could give to do this job. Sam shook his head and tromped across the fine layer of snow. More would be coming soon.

He wasn't sure he had it in him. He longed for the cool forest in summer, to be away from this place. Each time he thought of it, his heart sank a little.

Belinda was up ahead, her young boy in her arms, at the grave of her dead husband. His heart ached to see it. The wind tore at her hair, whipping it back and forth. A faint cry came with it, the boy.

He was cold, just like Sam.

Sam gnawed on his lip, looking at the door to the Keep. It would be warmer in there. He almost went to it when his feet seemed to change direction mid-stride. Her body was shivering. Sam took off his cloak. Now bare, his skin felt the full weight of the cold. He didn't care.

"You should take this." Sam offered it to her, a hand outstretched between them. She had sensed him coming or heard him, but stared hard at the grave marker.

"No."

"You can't be out here with this cold and that coat." There were huge gaps where the wind tore through her coat. It was threadbare.

"You won't have one."

"It was getting too warm out here, anyway." His teeth chattered as he said it. *How cold is it going to get this winter? Worse than last year?*

Last year had been filled with burning fires and cheery huts that beat back the cold at the end of the day. And warm food.

This winter, he wasn't so sure.

"Leave us."

"At least take it for the boy." She moved at that. Then, she turned her head. A hand snatched the coat away, and a few turns and twists later, the boy was wrapped in it.

Her eyes were clear as she looked at him, something other than hatred in them, he hoped.

"I will leave you to your mourning." Sam touched his head in respect, gave a quick glance to Archie's grave, and turned.

He strode away, not wanting to show how cold he was. He felt like crouching down, conserving as much heat as he could. Instead, he kept his back straight, unwilling to show a hint of weakness.

He left her, a widow on a hill mourning her husband, and wondered what would become of her.

9

ONE TO SEND FORTH

Sam stood over his bed. It was a new day, colder than the one before, and the snow was no longer a light dusting on the ground.

It had started the night before. He saw it through the windows, drifting down in large clumps. Every so often, one would come in and fall on the floor, then melt. How long until they had no heat at all?

"We aren't prepared for this," Ned said. "My bones can feel it. They ache, Sam."

Sam nodded. He didn't feel good either. The cold had set into him, settling down deep into his bones. Sometimes, he wondered if it would ever leave.

"The worst is yet to come, I imagine."

"We aren't going to survive the winter. I heard the ladies talking about how much food was left."

The others had gone off to their respective duties for the day. They were alone now, except for a young boy playing in the corner.

More weight. "There won't be enough to last, will there?"

"Not through winter, or spring."

"We're going to starve to death then." Sam straightened, then turned. "What can we do about it?" There was some irritation in his voice, and he saw it reflected in Ned's look.

"Nothing." Even in here, out of the worst of the wind and the cold, Ned shivered. Most of their winter wear had been burned up in the initial attack.

They needed fire. They needed warmth. *But what can I do about it?*

"I can't make food appear out of midair. I can't fill bellies with nothing but air." Sam felt his face pull into a scowl, and he tried to relax it.

"I didn't say you had to."

"Then why come to me about it?"

"Sometimes an old man needs a friend to talk to." Sadness filled his eyes, the corners wrinkled, and his eyebrows thick.

Shame struck Sam then. What had Ned done to deserve his condemnation, to deserve hard words?

He had been faithful, fought well, and always treated him with kindness and respect.

"I'm sorry, it's just..."

"We all have our burdens to bear. I wish yours was lighter."

"It feels like a mountain," Sam confessed. "Like a weight crushing me, pushing me down. There are..." He sought the right words.

"Rumors?"

Sam nodded.

"I've heard them too. It's hard not to." Ned sat down on the lumpy cloth that served as his bed, knees creaking and joints popping, and settled with a sigh. "They keep pestering me to join in that foolishness."

"What are we going to do about it?"

"Stay out of it, that's what." Ned leveled a hard gaze at him. "That's what I intend to do, and I suggest you do the same."

"But what if... it happens? Won't we be labeled as traitors and executed?"

"I assume so, unless we can plead our case." Ned scratched his beard, wispy and scraggly. "Like you said, though, we won't last long enough to see it."

"It doesn't seem right, him sitting there." Sam spoke softly. "Locked away behind that door while we suffer. It wouldn't be right to kill him, though."

"Imagine going through what he is. A life of ease and luxury taken away, sent to oversee a fortress being built under the noses of our worst enemies."

"Not a desirable position to be in." The scent of breakfast lingered in the air, a faint hint of the tasteless gruel that had become too normal.

The fireplace lay empty and bare, barely any ashes in it at all. Rogue snowflakes settled into the hearth, then melted.

"I wouldn't want to take his place." Ned moved, his body groaning in protest. "The others are coming in soon. Anything else to discuss?"

"Many more. How is Trent?" He hadn't seen him today. Even though Sam wasn't that busy, the hours seemed to slip by.

"He's a man."

"Not quite." He was young. Too young to be in a situation like this, but then Ned was too old to be in a situation like this.

No one should be in this castle at all. They should be out in the village, laughing and creating. Not waiting for their death.

"You don't give him enough credit. How was it that he held the walls?"

"Through his own skill." Sam remembered seeing him hold his own. Pride had blossomed in his chest at that, but also a great sadness that one so young could shed blood so easily.

And it reflected the thing inside him—so eager for violence, too ready to kill.

"And he's been invaluable to us since. He puts in the longest hours on the wall out of anyone, and more practice with the bow."

"You've been teaching him?"

Ned glanced at him from the corner of his eye. "Some."

"I haven't worked with him in weeks now. I should."

"Yes, you should. Teach him, Sam." Ned turned to him, imploring.

Sam shook his head slowly. "I don't think he wants me to."

"Nonsense."

"I haven't talked to him much since that day on the tower." Sam told the story quickly, rushing at the memory of the look of disappointment.

"I don't think he thinks you're a coward, not after the attack." Ned stretched his hands. How many things had those hands done, wrinkled and scarred? "You proved that to everyone, taking on that giant."

"And almost dying." He rubbed his arms, still sore from the beating that man gave him.

"Lesser men would have died earlier, and brave men would have cowered. They did." Men were starting to come back now, trickling in and talking among themselves. "We can talk about it more later."

One of the men yawned. Like Ned, they were coming off the night watch. "I'll leave you to rest. Get some sleep." Sam stood, but Ned caught his arm.

"Talk to him. Today, if you can."

"I've got a lot to do." Sam tightened his coat in preparation for the cold. He could feel Ned's gaze on him as he walked away.

Snow was drifting down, adding to the few inches of white that already carpeted the castle. Thankfully, there was no wind, and Sam stepped outside with reluctance.

The Keep didn't offer a warm bastion against the cold, but it did offer some protection. Out in the yard, he could feel it.

It started at his feet, worse at his exposed hands and head. The ground pulled the heat out of his feet and seemed to drain it from the rest of his body.

He followed footsteps that were being covered up. Men walked along the castle walls, pacing along the battlements with a keen eye to the south.

Sam knew they wouldn't attack now. There was too much snow. Even if the Belmarchers could get across the plain in front of the walls, they would have a tough time scaling the walls, ladders or not.

No, they would dig in and wait them out. Sam wondered if they could launch a counterattack, take them by surprise.

He ran through the number of fighters they had within the walls, then the number of fighters that were camped outside.

It would be suicide, and the attackers wouldn't last long. He was more confident about the men now, but he still wasn't sure they could do anything other than keep the attackers away.

The tracks split—some to the forge, some to the masons, some to the carpenter's workshop. Sam chose to follow the ones to the mason's area, the most used out of all of them.

It was going to be a hard time, and he knew it, but Sam had to do this. Tired, hungry, and afraid of the confrontation that awaited him, Sam walked through the rough stone walls of the new mason's workshop.

Hammers were striking chisels, the masons chipping away at the worst of the stone. Bill was in the corner, lounging in a chair. From where he had gotten it, Sam didn't know.

The masons went silent as Sam stood there, the air thick with the dust of the stone. Gray chips littered the floor like sawdust, and they crunched underfoot.

"Sam Freeman, come to see me in my natural habitat?" Bill stood up and grinned, completely at ease. He was surrounded by ten or fifteen of his masons, so it wasn't surprising.

"If you can spare it." There wasn't the air of hostility Sam was expecting, or would have encountered just a few months ago. Walking in unannounced then would have been... foolish.

But now, there was a hint of respect, even among the masons Bill had worked so hard to turn against him.

It was surprising and, Sam wondered, refreshing. Almost heady.

That scared him the most. "May we talk in private?"

Bill nodded to the mason by his side and motioned to follow as he stood. "Keep up the work, boys."

Sam crunched across the room, stepping around the rock pedestals they were using as workbenches. The hammers resumed, and chips continued to fall once again.

They were cutting off the worst of the jutting sections of rock, the sharp points that would interfere with a good grip. Layers of rough rock came in one end of the workshop, and the smoothed, prepared rock went out the other.

Bill had taken his time thinking through the layout, for Sam was certain it came under his direction. That, or he took good advice.

Sam noted that and entered into a small shack outside and around the corner. It was dark inside, tucked up against the wall that made up one side of it, with a small window that overlooked the yard and the snow that hushed the world.

"I see you've come around to my idea."

Sam took a deep breath, preparing for what was to come. "No." Bill frowned, but didn't look too surprised. "But I've thought of something else."

"And what, pray tell, is that?"

"The crane." Bill looked at him blankly.

"Am I supposed to guess? I don't have time or patience for games," Bill said.

"The Golden River will take a message for us. Or, rather, a messenger."

It had been in his mind for a while now, since before the attack. The Belmarch had set up too good a defense to get anyone out the now-ruined gates. And, if they did, Sam wasn't sure they wouldn't end up like the last messenger.

If they did, then that was another life wasted.

"I'm listening." Bill sat on the stone bench that seemed to function as his desk. Sam joined him on the opposite side. It was cold, and sucked the heat from him.

"We can move a crane, take it from the tower since we aren't going to finish it anyway, and put it on the wall that abuts the river. I think we have enough room, if we can position it right, to swing a boat out over the river."

"Once we do that, we add a person, send them down and around the Belmarch, and get help."

"Interesting. Why come to me about this?" Bill rubbed his fingers together, making Sam aware of how cold his hands were.

"Two reasons. I need your help to set the crane in the wall. Stone will need to come out, and I'm not sure we can make it unless we take out a merlon."

"And the second?"

"I need you to convince the Overseer to let us do it. He isn't going to listen to me."

"Who will go on this boat?" Bill's brows furrowed. "We don't have a boat."

"We can take care of that." Sam hid his fear that they might not have enough wood left to make it. "By the time we get it ready, we'll have a functional boat."

"Have you ever built a boat?" Before Sam could answer, Bill went on. "Never mind. Let's take a walk. I want to see it."

They left, walking across the fresh snow that compressed beneath their feet. "And the messenger?" Bill asked when they were far enough to be out of earshot. "Who did you have in mind?"

"I didn't. It would have to be someone who could convince the King to come."

"Perhaps the Duke himself?" Bill mused, almost to himself. "I'll have to think on that. There are some good candidates." Sam stared at him out of the corner of his eye. *What is he planning? And have I become an unwilling participant in it?*

There was no doubt that with the masons behind him, Bill was the most dangerous man in the castle, but the Overseer still had control of the guard, and the weapons.

"This is the closest point," Sam said, stopping at the location he had in mind. The waters of the Golden River flowed beneath them, rushing by. It was fast, which would take a boat past the enemy quickly. "I haven't seen any of their sentries focused on the river either." Sam had asked to be put on this wall during his watches.

Bill leaned out over the edge, judging the distance, and then examined the wall. "I think we could do it. The crane will fit, for sure, but I think you're right."

A trick of relief flowed through Sam. It was reassuring to hear after thinking about it so long and hard.

"Take out a few here, and we can demolish this," Bill put his hand on the merlon. "Maybe the one next to it to get some space to swing the crane over."

"And the boat," Sam reminded him.

"The boat too. How long is it?"

"Not sure yet." That was something Ned was going to have to lead. Sam had no idea how to build anything that floated.

"I could see this working." Bill stared downriver. "We could get help." The snow obscured their visibility, and they couldn't even see the other bank. "But I have a condition."

The glint in his eye made Sam reconsider what he'd just asked. "What is it?" he asked, wary of the response.

"I get to choose who leaves."

10

AN EXCHANGE

Sam stood in the falling snow on the wall, examining Bill. The wiry man was hiding his intentions well. Sam couldn't read him.

He thought about the proposal. "Is that the only condition?"

"That's it. I'll help you build your crane, and work it too, if you need it."

Sam had expected something else, a promise extracted or a favor that would be hard to swallow. He couldn't help thinking there was some ulterior motive driving Bill's thought process.

But, for the life of him, he couldn't figure it out. It was getting colder now, and the light of day was growing stronger. There might be an end to the snow soon.

His thoughts wandered to the Belmarch lands. Since they were to the north, they had to be used to the cold—if not better suited to it. Had their attackers come prepared for the bitter winter ahead?

Maybe there was another reason they had stopped attacking.

He breathed deep of the fresh, crisp air, cleansed of anything by the snow. He had never smelled anything cleaner.

"I hope I don't regret this." Sam held out his hand, and Bill took it. His grip was iron, and they sealed the pact.

"How soon are you planning this?"

"Give me some time. I've got a boat to build."

Bill nodded. "Don't take too long. I'll go see Rhys and work on him. Drop a few hints."

"Make it sound like it was your idea, and I know he'll say yes."

"You make me more powerful than I really am." Bill spread his arms out and gave a small shrug. "I'm just a humble mason."

Sam snorted. "You're nothing of the sort." Bill grinned and bid him goodbye, sauntering to the Keep.

Sam looked out over the river, trying to pierce the snowfall. That direction lay their salvation.

He hoped they would get to it in time.

***

The workshop was freezing when Sam entered. He blew air into his cupped hands, which looked an alarming pale color. Ned, Trent, and Kerien were there working.

Or trying to. It was cold, and all of them were shivering. If only they had material to make coats.

But where would that come from? The nonexistent animals? The river reeds below?

The thought struck him like a lightning bolt. Maybe they could use the crane for more than just a message.

They might be able to use it as a way to sneak out of the castle during the night, collect much-needed supplies.

His fingers tingled—not just from warming up, but from the excitement running through his body.

"What is it?" Ned stopped, his saw poised to cut through a board. "You look like the siege has been lifted."

"No," Sam said, taking a deep breath to get control of his body. "We need to build a boat. Ned, I'm going to need your help."

The carpenters looked at each other, then back at him as if he had sprouted wings and was floating in midair.

"A boat?" Ned said finally.

"What do we need a boat for?" Kerien asked.

"I've got a plan." Sam ran through his idea quickly, leaving out the promised favor to Bill.

In the worst case, he would pick the Duke, which might be the best option. Best case would be another mason, one familiar with the paths back to the capital.

One thing kept nagging him, though. Who would believe them? And, even if they were believed, what kind of aid could they possibly send?

They must know something was wrong by now. The shipment of supplies and men was supposed to arrive before winter set in.

Unless they had left too late, or were captured or killed along the way. Then, they wouldn't expect them back until later.

However Sam looked at it, their chances were not good.

"It could work," Trent said. The boy was harder than he had been, and looked stronger, but thinner.

"It's been a while since I've even worked on boats." Ned rubbed his bushy eyebrows and stroked his beard. "I don't know..."

"We don't have much choice, do we?" Sam asked.

"It's not like we're doing anything better anyway. Stupid Belmarchers haven't attacked in weeks." Sam was surprised to hear a measure of support from Kerien. "Besides, I learned boat building during my apprenticeship."

They turned to him. Kerien shrugged. "I never thought to bring it up before. It didn't seem important."

"That... is a good surprise," Sam said. "That means we have two boat builders."

Ned shook his head. "One and a half, at best."

"So, what do we need to do then?"

"Look through the stock," Kerien said, turning to the wood stacked in the corner, blessedly safe from the snow.

"Agreed." Ned joined him.

***

A few hours later, they had combed through everything and segregated the wood that they would use for the boat.

Ned stood over it, arms crossed, with a frown on his face. "It isn't enough."

It looked like a healthy pile to Sam.

"Why not?" Trent asked.

"We'll use most of it making the curves. There isn't enough bent stock." Sam groaned. They had sorted out the best, straightest stock to haul into the castle, and some of the other wood had been burned long ago for warmth.

"So we're back to square one." Sam sat back, leaning against his workbench. "This is going to be a problem."

He knew this point would come without a forest of trees to draw on. Even if they could suddenly go out and fell a few more, it would be months before they were ready and dry enough to use.

"We could join some together," Trent said.

Ned shook his head. "It would be leaky as it is. We don't have the pitch to seal the joints we're going to have to put in, let alone adding more."

"I've heard and seen it happen." Kerien's face went grim. "The one time we did it was bad—it sank the boat next to the dock. Luckily, the water was shallow."

"Was anyone hurt?" Trent asked, eyes wide.

"No, it was overnight, so no one was in it."

"It took that long?" Sam leaned back, thinking. "If we can't make it watertight, what are we going to do?"

"Give whoever is riding in it a bucket." Ned took the biggest piece they had. "We'll get started, if you can handle the rest of the work."

By the rest of the work, he really meant the arrow-making. They had enough bows to comfortably outfit almost all the men. Enough to give the Belmarchers pause if they tried a frontal assault again.

Even now, Sam thought they were lulling them into a sense of complacency. The sentries could only hold out so long before they started paying less attention.

He had seen it—men staring off into the distance on the wall as he walked by, or looking in the courtyard to watch the young ones play. If that was their strategy, the Belmarchers were winning.

But winter had come, and with it ice and snow, horrible conditions to try and scale a wall or break open a gate. Though the ground might be hard because it was frozen, it was also slippery.

That gave him another idea, and Sam tucked it away in his memory for later use.

"Can you make do for now, until we find another way?" Sam asked.

Kerien and Ned talked it over, then agreed. "Yes, we'll start with this."

Another problem to fix, in the now ever-growing line of them. It seemed like every time he solved one, another popped up.

Somewhere in the back of his mind, Sam was curious about the pile of planks. They were straight, not that wide, and thin. There were a few offcuts that were chunkier, but nothing that resembled a boat.

How were they going to get all those straight lines into a curved boat?

He was a little afraid of the answer, so he kept the question to himself. This was not his expertise. Let them work unhindered. I have work to do.

He couldn't remember the last time he had felt ready to work, but he still forced himself to return to his workbench and let the others go.

He turned to making arrows, splitting them off the edge of one of the smaller boards.

It was still green, the rough bark on two edges. The curve of the grain traveled up the edge, but he wasn't sure if it twisted.

A few cuts from his plane removed the dirty endgrain. It was all sapwood, oak. A faint trace of pungent odor from the fresh cut end refreshed him.

Kerien and Ned were talking over the boat construction, picking over the pieces and arranging them in a suitable manner.

It went on the rest of the day, but Sam couldn't get into his work. He was distracted and kept making errors. Each time, he would slow down and refocus, only to be distracted again.

Lunch came and went, if you could call a meager portion of whatever was in the pot a meal, and the afternoon light quickly faded as the evening came over them.

"The days are getting short," Ned said, squinting at his handiwork. He was shaving the biggest piece down with a chisel. "Less time for work."

Sam frowned, seeing how dark it was getting. Candles, or even the fire, would have kept them going in the darkness. It would have provided light and warmth.

But they didn't have enough candles to spare, and even less wood to burn.

"We'll work for another half hour."

"When are we supposed to finish this?" Kerien asked.

"As soon as possible. Yesterday, if we could."

"Then someone should have thought of that sooner." Kerien's face darkened, the corners of his mouth pulled down. "Why can't anyone think of what we need ahead of time?" With each word, the volume of his voice grew, until it seemed he was shouting.

"Watch your tongue," Sam warned.

"No. I won't." Kerien threw down the chunk of wood he was holding. It clattered on his workbench, then fell to the floor without a sound.

Anger flashed up inside Sam, fueled by the conditions and the pressure. He held it back, though, even though he was tired of Kerien acting out like a child.

Instead of saying something else, Sam took a deep breath. Tension filled the air, and Trent was staring at him with wide eyes. No one said anything for a while.

Kerien looked like he wanted to fight, tense and ready. He rocked forward onto the balls of his feet.

Sam could have fought him then, but there was no point. He would have won, but then he would have given Kerien what he asked for. Practicality begging for it.

"Go somewhere else tonight," Sam finally said, keeping his voice down.

"I know it's a hard time right now," Ned said, stepping forward and partially blocking the way between them. "We look outside and see the bleak winter and the enemy surrounding us."

"How will we survive if we can't work together? How will we get out of this and live to see another day?" Sam wasn't sure he wanted to be around Kerien right now. He wasn't sure Kerien would survive long enough to see the Belmarch attack again.

"Yes, we must work together," Sam said woodenly. The words came out, but they were forced.

Kerien turned and left the workshop, rushing out into the gloom of the night. Sam was glad, even though his entire body was quivering with anger.

"It's been hard on him too," Ned whispered, walking up to him. "He hasn't had anyone to turn to."

"Turn to?" Sam stared at him.

There was sorrow beneath Ned's bushy eyebrows. "He and Archie were closer than you knew. They were like brothers."

The anger dissipated, cut through to the bone with those words. Sam stared at him. "I... didn't think about that."

Ned smiled a gaunt smile. "He doesn't show it much, but it's always a constant reminder whenever he's around the workshop. Archie helped him as an apprentice."

"They apprenticed together?"

"No, Kerien was apprenticed at the same master that Archie was working for years ago. He showed him a spot of kindness in a sea of trouble and pain."

"Pain?"

"He had a hard master. He beat Kerien whenever he made a mistake, or went too slow, or even went too fast."

"How do you know this?"

Ned shrugged. "People talk to me. Or around me. Not the same as around you. He looks up to you."

Sam hadn't even stopped to consider it. Ned patted him on the shoulder and followed.

Maybe he had been too hard on Kerien, hadn't spoken enough soft words.

It was too late for that now, and Sam felt the emptiness of it deep in his stomach.

11

CONVERSATION IN THE COLD

Trent lingered in the workshop and fidgeted with a few arrows.

Sam felt mixed up and horrible for what Ned had revealed to him. To have been so blind, to have not seen why Kerien was so angry.

The workshop was where they had spent most of their time together. True, that was the workshop outside the gates, but even here, Archie had left his mark.

Archie's workbench was cold and lifeless. A spiderweb shivered in the breeze beneath it, and dust and sawdust coated the tools there.

Sam thought they were untouched, but when he looked closer, he realized that they were lined up in a neat row, uncharacteristically. Archie never kept his tools neat like that.

But Kerien did.

Was that part of his mourning process, and the reason he couldn't let go?

Near the door, Trent cleared his throat. It broke Sam's thoughts, and he turned.

What am I supposed to say? "How are you?" Sam said, settling for the least cringe-inducing thing he could think of.

"They're treating me better. Bill, and the others, I mean."

"I knew what you meant." He was so young in Sam's eyes. Just a boy.

"I have you to thank for that." Trent's eyes dropped to the ground. "I know I haven't been the most grateful apprentice, and I want to change that."

It surprised him. Gone was the strange look, one of almost hate, that Trent once bore for him. He hadn't noticed it before, but once he said that, it was obvious.

"I haven't been the best master either. For that, I am sorry."

"You taught me to fight, and that kept me alive."

"It did more than keep you alive." Sam moved closer, the light almost completely gone. He wished there was a candle he could light, a place where they could go to see each other.

But then, he wasn't sure Trent would be able to talk to him if there was.

I have been a poor master and an even worse teacher. Sam hadn't really talked to him since the last attack, the one that took Archie's life. That was days ago, weeks even. He hadn't taught him anything, hadn't trained him.

Sam had been so caught up in everything around him, he had almost forgotten Trent even needed him.

"I think I took it for granted that you were learning so fast," Sam said. "You've made more progress in these last few months than any I've seen."

Trent, even in the darkness, seemed to swell. "I have a confession to make." Trent seemed to be waiting for something, for Sam expected him to say something.

Instead, he heard Trent squirming in the dark. It gave Sam time to prepare himself, thinking of the worst. Had Trent found out his secret past? That was absurd, considering who he was. Then, what was it?

Perhaps Trent had talked to Bill, was going to join him in his deadly plans. What if Bill had convinced him to be the one to do it, to kill the Duke?

"I—I thought you were a coward," Trent said at last.

Sam cocked his head, waiting for more. When none came, he couldn't help but laugh. "That's it?"

"I'm sorry for it. You aren't."

"Trent, I knew you thought that about me. Let's go outside." It was too dark to talk at all in the workshop, and Sam pushed open the flap, letting starlight flood through.

Night was in full regalia now, stars shining and twinkling up above in a clear, cold sky. The wind was dead as they left the workshop behind.

"You knew? The whole time? Why didn't you say anything?"

Sam shrugged. "If I would have said something, would it have changed your mind?"

"Yes, it would have," Trent said, pulling his arms around himself in a hug against the cold.

"Only action got you to change your mind about me, and that action was spurned by another."

"What other?"

"You." The smell of woodsmoke drifted through the air. Trent looked confused. "When I saw you fighting on the walls, it made me think back to what I had sworn long ago and consider it again."

"I had sworn never to do violence again on my enemies." Sam shook his head, feeling his forehead tighten. "But I never considered that there would be others who would fight in my stead, especially one as young as you." Trent listened keenly.

"I realized that it would be a cowardly thing indeed to abandon my friends, those I love, and not fight when I have the skill and ability. I couldn't let you fight alone, while I refused to do anything."

Sam looked up at the sky. The Deer and the Boar were low on the horizon, followed by the Hunter. Winter had truly begun, and the Raven was halfway visible above them.

Four months. Four more months of this, at least. Maybe longer.

"That's what drove me to fight, and I've been thinking about it ever since." Sam shivered in the night air.

"I miss our nights of training," Trent said. They crunched through the snow, the top layer cracking from where it had melted and refrozen. "They saved me too. I couldn't have fought without you teaching me. Will you teach me again?"

Sam smiled. There was something warming about the thought, that he hadn't messed everything up like he had feared. A wave of relief washed through him.

He hadn't expected it. Sam hadn't expected the glimmer in Trent's eyes either, reflecting the starlight so subtly.

The Keep grew before them. They would be there in a few more steps. Sam didn't have much time alone with him, and it was too cold to linger.

"I'd be honored to teach you more," Sam said. "After dinner, we'll train." He was going to do better. Sam couldn't change the past, but he could do something about the future.

"I'm not looking forward to dinner," Trent said after he nodded. His teeth chattered in the cold.

"To be honest, neither am I." Sam knew he should have been happy they had food, but the same over and over again. It wasn't going to get better anytime soon, either.

Yet another reason to get that messenger to the capital. Bill's favor hung over him, then he thought about something he hadn't before.

What if Bill chose me to go?

He tried to push it to the side, but the thought lodged a sliver of dread within him, not over the act of leaving itself, but of leaving everyone else alone with Bill. No matter what he said, Sam still wasn't sure about him or his intentions.

"Let's go inside," Sam said. He pushed open the creaking doors and stepped out of the wind behind Trent. The bell sounded, beckoning them to dinner.

Compared to outside, the wave of warm air that greeted him felt glorious. He let it wash over his face, bringing some life back into his cheeks. They burned as the blood came back to them.

Everyone else was eating. There was little conversation, but enough to make a hum in the air.

The days of laughter were gone, and Sam felt it all the more keenly now. Would laughter ever grace the halls again? He wasn't sure.

He wasn't even sure the great fireplace would ever see fire again.

Seeing them there, he was reminded of just how hopeless their plight was. Even if they were to survive the winter alive, without dying of starvation, the Belmarch army would surely arrive come spring.

And they would not hold back from attacking, of that Sam was certain. They would break through the wall or the gate, and they would slaughter them one by one.

Unless they had help, they would certainly die. And they could not work in the night, not without squandering their resources.

It was beyond frustrating. He needed more men working, he needed more supplies. And where was the Duke? Still holed up in his quarters, enjoying the best of what they had left. He even had a fire going, probably.

Belinda was sitting with her child, feeding him the evening gruel. He was eating it, but didn't seem to be enjoying it. Sam followed Trent up to get his food, which was dispensed without a word by a sorry-faced woman. She seemed depressed.

He wanted to say something kind, but all he could muster was "Thank you."

Her eyes flashed up to his for a second, then fell back. She sat back in her seat for her own meal, spooning it up in a big glob.

Sam joined the other carpenters, eating by the light of the moon and stars. It was difficult, and unappetizing, food to eat. The third bell rang, and the men finished their meal. Those destined for the first night watch went to the side of the hall filled with beds to sleep in, while the others went back into the cold.

The practice weapons were handed out, the men complaining bitterly of the cold. Sam wanted to join them but knew that things were about to change.

There was an energy in him when he reached into his cloak and pulled out Yand's old weapon. It had been next to his body the whole time, he slipped it there after dinner, and it was warm.

It traveled up his arm and into his soul. A part of him loved the thrill, loved the anticipation.

And yet, there was that other part that loved something else. The part of him that scared him, that he detested. The dark part of him that smiled when bone crunched and flesh tore.

He tried to bury that part of him as he took up his place next to the guards. Even in the dark of night, the questioning glances showed up on the faces of the others, and whispers ran through the crowd.

"From here on out, we're going to change how things are done." Sam's voice rang out above the whispers, silencing them. "We're going to focus on the basic moves you'll need to survive and nothing else. We don't have the time to do otherwise."

"We survived this far, haven't we?" someone asked, voice lost in the crowd. Sam had anticipated this.

"You did well during the last attack. You stood your ground like true men of Chathem." He paused and looked around. "But I suspect the next time we're attacked, it won't be a simple raiding party twice our number, but an army thirty times our number. Can you fight them off then?"

Gasps and whispers erupted at his exclamation. The men started talking. Sam held up his hands, trying to get control back. "Listen."

Mathew joined him, along with the other guards, echoing his command.

The talking died down. "You can listen to lies if you'd like, but I've chosen to tell you the truth. Is there any other man with experience in battle who will step forward? He is more than welcome to take my place."

Sam waited, watching his breath freeze into puffs of air in the faint moonlight. When he turned his head, the snow on the ground caught it, shimmering.

He waited some more. No one came forward. More than half of him wanted someone to do it, to take it away.

He would gladly give it up, return to the life of creation instead of destruction. He didn't know for sure that he was the only one that felt that way, only suspected it from seeing them fight.

Even the guards had done a middling job of fighting, at best.

But he waited in vain. A few men coughed, more shuffled and stamped their feet in the cold, trying to stay warm.

He waited some more, until the silence was uncomfortable. No one was going to do it. Even Bill was standing, looking anywhere but at Sam.

That gave him some hope. If Bill truly wanted to enact an uprising, taking control of the fighting training would have been a good place to start.

"No one? None of you will meet my challenge?" Sam said, voice raised. He lowered it, still loud enough so that they could hear, but have to strain to do so.

"Fine. Let us begin."

12

BACK TO THE BASICS

After less than an hour of training, almost all the men in the yard were sweating. Considering how cold it was outside, Sam was satisfied.

"That's enough," he said.

"That's it?" Mathew asked. "We train more than this normally."

Sam had run them through strength training, striking, and defense. They'd even got a few rounds of sparring in.

"It's enough. We don't have the food to recover our strength if we push too hard."

"I hadn't thought of that." Mathew turned and nodded to the other guards.

Sam stretched his muscles, which were yelling at him. It was a good feeling, all the way down to his legs and calves. He knew that tomorrow they would be sore, but for now, it wasn't too bad.

His old wounds, mostly healed, flared up in pain again. He had pushed too hard tonight.

The guards dismissed the group, each squad leader taking aside his respective squad to give them the night's orders. Sam joined his squad and felt awkward as Verith went through the watch assignments, then dismissed them.

Sam kept an eye on Trent, who had done well during the training. He was picking up the sword fast—faster than anyone Sam had seen in a long time. Trent had even put a few others to shame in the sparring sessions.

Sam watched for signs of hostility or darker behavior he suspected might be lurking against Trent, but he saw none. A joke was passed, and the group laughed quickly before dispersing. Trent stood shoulder to shoulder with them, steam rising off his shoulders like the rest.

"You did well tonight," Sam said, approaching him. "But I'm afraid you can't do any more tonight. We have the second watch, so you'll need to rest before."

"I understand. There's always tomorrow."

"Tomorrow it is. Meet me after training, and we'll go through a few forms I think you're ready for."

They were at the Keep now, and slipped inside its cool halls. Men were slipping into their beds, nothing else to do without light.

"Goodnight, Trent."

"Goodnight."

Sam unfolded his nightclothes—just another set of clothes that was wearing thin, and slipped under his thin blanket.

He didn't sleep well and was soon awakened for his watch. Sam stumbled out of bed, shivering in the cold, and put on as many of his clothes as he could.

He headed to the guardhouse, meeting the others. He took the bow and arrows issued to him and took up position on the south wall as directed.

Sam knew he could have changed locations, but he wanted to watch the Belmarch and their camp.

The night was clear and calm, any hint of cloud cover gone. The moon hung in a shallow crescent just behind him, the tip of it touching the top of the unfinished Keep.

The Belmarch had sentries patrolling. They weren't relax-ing, he even spotted a few near the forest edge.

They're prepared for us to do something.

They didn't go anywhere near the river, as far as he could tell. The bare branches stretched into the night sky like bony fingers reaching up from a grave.

That dread crept into him again as he considered his fate. He could join Archie tonight if the Belmarch attacked. Whether by arrow or blade, they could end his life.

And what kind of life would end? A miserable existence in a half-finished castle? The pain of hunger in his belly he had known before, and he knew would only grow deeper.

Sam closed his eyes for a moment. He had wanted peace, quiet in his life after a less-than-peaceful childhood.

Then why did you come here? It slipped into his mind, making him snap open his eyes. He had come here to build, to create, to make.

Not to fight.

The thing inside him stirred. It had been asleep for too long and wanted to wake up. Sam, deep down inside, needed to tear and rend flesh, make others feel pain, the pain that he had felt.

No. Sam tightened his freezing fingers on the unstrung bow. *I have done enough killing.*

Then why did you come here, almost to the heart of enemy country? A bloodthirsty, savage enemy.

Sam knew why he did it. It wasn't just to build. He had always known there was a chance of conflict, and there in the cold of the night, he had to confront himself about it.

All the while the enemy was safe in warm huts, a comfort-able camp. This was the life he had always resisted, but one he knew he would return to.

"How long do I need to do this?" Sam's voice was quiet in the darkness, a whisper. "How long am I going to keep living this life?"

The thing within him coiled tighter, stirring from sleep.

A snowflake landed on his head, then another. The sky that had been clear an hour or so ago was now filled with clouds and snow. The bitter cold had receded with its arrival, but hadn't gone away.

Sam felt a snowflake land on his cheek and melt away to nothing. *That is my life*. A moment, formed like ice, then gone. Nothing left except a trail of water, which would soon disappear.

Evan was more than restless now. He paced his room, chewing on the end of his thumb. He had ordered Rhys to keep the wine away from him and was regretting every second of it.

He was caged like an animal, trapped in a prison of cold and damp. They wouldn't let him have a fire anymore, even though it was winter and cold. Rhys had barely given him a candle, despite his protests.

Claimed there were too few left to waste. He didn't know what that fool was saying, light was no waste for the Duke of Hornblood.

His last ration of candle was down to the nub, just like his thumb would be if he didn't stop chewing it.

There was nothing to do but wait for Rhys. His eyes wandered to the bookshelf. Evan had always considered it superfluous—ornamentation to make him look better. He didn't consider reading any of the books it contained.

And it had a few, a small fortune in its own. Nowhere else in the castle had them. It was his library, given by the generosity of his family.

He went over to it, stuck a finger on the spine of one. It came away filthy.

Evan pulled out a book and blew the dust from the top.

Never much of a reader, he didn't see the use in books. He pulled one out and read the title: *History of Chathem.*

He dropped it on his desk, staring up again at the enormous crest above it. Having it there was a burden and a reminder, and he was sorry it witnessed his breakdown.

If Yand were here, what would he counsel?

Evan knew Yand wouldn't tell him to sit there and do nothing, but Yand hadn't been well-versed in politics and suspected Yand wouldn't have much to say on the matter except to use force.

But Evan had no forces loyal to him at the moment, according to what Rhys said and implied, other than through him to the guard. Less than a dozen men now, after the attack.

His fist clenched into a ball and he struck the desk. *Blast that resupply, where was it?*

It was supposed to be here months ago, and included the rest of his luggage. His father hadn't let him take more with him, promising that he would send it soon.

In truth, he knew that it was the other supplies they needed more. The food and tools and weapons that were planned to fortify it. More men, more workers, what little they had been able to recruit to go north. Few men had wanted to make that trip, even if they would be able to take their families.

And now he too knew the reason. It was too dangerous, that was what the advisers had said, that they were doing their best. Their best wasn't good enough. If it had been, Evan would have marched to Hornblood with a hundred men-at-arms ready to garrison it and a hundred craftsman to make it whole.

Instead, he was sitting in a moldering, festering ruin with no way to get out and no hope of escape.

"Improve yourself first, then you can work on others." That was what Yand had said on more than one occasion when he had been caught out or returned home drunk.

So how am I supposed to do that in here? Evan paced around again, taking yet another lap around his room. The walls were suffocating.

He had to do something. Dinner was still hours away.

He made up his mind. Yand had taught him to fight—he would practice. Evan pushed the table and chairs back against the wall, giving himself enough room to move freely. He practiced his breathing, then moved into his forms.

The sword came out of the scabbard with a whisper of steel, and a slight ring that echoed through the room. The hilt felt cold in his hands, but the sword was balanced well. It was a joy to swing, and doing it brought back memories of days in the practice yard, covered in dust and sweat and bruises, but that were the best times of his life.

He felt alive then, like he did when he was sneaking into an inn as a commoner and drinking their bravest souls under the table.

Lunges first, then parries. Evan went through all the basic forms. He was rusty, not having practiced since Yand had forced him to on their arrival. He kept making mistakes and had to go back through them all again.

"Focus on the forms," Yand's voice echoed in his memory. *"Don't try to be fancy."*

So he focused on the forms. He ran through them until he had them smooth again, then ran through them again. He went through the forms, forgetting everything else in the world, pouring his thoughts and desires into his muscles.

Before he knew it there was a knock on his door. He was covered in sweat, and his arms were shaking from holding his sword for so long. Evan caught his breath, then let the servant in with dinner. He wolfed it down, then returned to his practice.

The candle flickered and went out, but he kept going. In the darkness he was able to concentrate more, feel the forms as they flowed through him.

His arms started shaking, then his legs, but there was no desire to drink anything. It had been banished by pain and effort that flowed through him.

Finally, it was too much for him to bear. The sword clattered out of his grip and onto the stone floor.

He stood, panting, and then leaned over his desk to catch his breath. What would Yand think of him now? He wasn't sure, but he knew it wouldn't be bad.

He couldn't see in the dark more than faint outlines in the small amount of moonlight that came in the window near the ceiling, but he knew that crest was up there.

For the first time in a while, maybe ever, he stood under it and felt that maybe, just maybe, it wasn't so imposing than he first thought.

13

UNDISCOVERED

Evan woke late the next morning. His body was screaming at him with soreness and his arms were so stiff he could hardly move them. Sunlight poured in his window, and bathed him in a warm glow as he tried to bend his elbows. Pain shot up his arms, and he groaned. Knocking on his door made him sit up, and made his body throb with soreness.

"Come in," he said, managing to raise his voice enough to be heard. It was the one part of him that didn't seem to be aching.

Overseer Rhys cracked the door and peeked inside. His face smoothed as soon as he saw Evan, hiding something.

"Good morning, Highness."

"Is it still morning?"

"Yes. I've come to go over the figures with you. You weren't in your office, so I thought..."

"I'm not drunk, if that's what you're asking," Evan said, trying to slide his legs to the edge of the bed. He groaned again.

"The thought never entered my mind." Rhys furrowed his eyebrows and set down his bundle of records. "Do you need help? I can call the servants."

Evan almost went white with shame. What would everyone think if they had to drag him out of bed like this? "No," he snapped. "I can manage," he said, in a kinder tone.

"Very well." Rhys cocked his head as Evan tried to struggle to his feet, falling back. *How did my toes get this sore?*

Rhys grabbed one of his parchments. "Perhaps it would be better to go over this here?" he asked with an arched brow.

Evan dreaded the short walk to his office. It was next door, but it might as well have been in the capital.

"Why don't you start here, and we'll see how it goes." Evan was bending some life back into his body, one finger at a time. Yand always recommended moving after a hard training session, and Evan went through his limbering form.

"Starting with the inventory," Rhys said, pausing for him to nod. When he did Rhys continued. "As for food stores, we are—"

"Before that," Evan said, cutting him off. There was something bothering him even more than the food. "Tell me about the... conditions out there."

Rhys rolled up his parchment and set it back on the table. He had sat down while Evan was trying to bring his body to life, which had been somewhat successful. At least now it didn't hurt like he was being cooked.

After a short pause, Rhys folded his hands. "I wish I could report better news, but not much has changed."

Not much. Evan was hoping it had died down, or that everything was a big joke and that he could go outside again. The sliver of light from his windows wasn't' enough of the world for him.

"How has it changed?"

Rhys shifted in his seat, but his face remained expressionless. The man was a true politician and seemed to be able to hide what he was thinking with ease.

Evan didn't like that. Not one bit.

"I'm working to ease the situation. Unfortunately, as you'll soon discover, there isn't much in the way of goods to do it."

"What do we do, then?"

"I'm not sure, Your Highness."

Evan closed his eyes, trying to process everything. His father would know what to do in a situation like this. Oh how he wished he had a man, or beast, to send to him now.

"And I can't go outside to help at all?" Evan asked.

"I'm not sure what good it will do."

"It will show my face—remind them who walks the Keep and who will inherit this place."

"Would that be better, or worse, for the situation?" Rhys was calm. *Expecting an outburst?*

Evan didn't blame him if he was. Even now, his anger was rising. But who was to blame? Rhys? Yand? His father? Or was it his own actions—his own stupidity—that had led him to this road he now had to travel alone?

"I'm not cut out for these games, Rhys. It doesn't suit me."

"I will try my best to help you." He reached out and patted Evan's hand, what appeared to be a sincere look of pain and pity on his face. "But I've never been in this kind of situation either, I'm afraid."

Despite his soreness, Evan straightened his back, pulling himself up. "I'll try to do my best then, if I can do anything at all." He licked his dry, parched lips. "Let's get on with the inventory then."

Rhys nodded and took out his records. "We're down to three months' worth of dry goods. All of the fresh vegetables are gone, as well as the meats."

That explains the lack of variety in the meals.

"Do we have any way of getting more food?" Evan buried his head in his hands.

"The birds have all migrated south for the winter. I would have told you we could catch a few, but that won't be true in this weather. We have nothing planted within the walls of the castle."

"So our only hope is to get resupplied by someone else. Like my father."

"Or the King, if I can get a message to him," Rhys said.

"Or the King," Evan repeated. Great, just have to get a message to him through this attacking army that killed our last messenger. "What about the river?"

"I don't know what you mean."

"Could they resupply us by the river?" Evan asked.

Rhys wrinkled his brow. "I suppose so, except they would have to go by the gate."

"Then that's out too." Evan sighed and leaned back on his hands. It burned his shoulders, but felt good to get some relief off his lower back, it was killing him.

A *source of life and an easy way to travel.* Evan had expected to use it more than it had been.

"Do we risk another messenger through the woods, then? Or try to break out before the Belmarch can fortify their position?" Evan wondered aloud, not expecting much of an answer. Rhys was a politician, not a tactician.

"My reports say the Belmarch keep up their sentries in the forest and have enough men to stay on watch all night," Rhys grimaced. "Who would be the one to send if we could?"

"So we sit here and wait. Hope that my father finds out on his own." Evan's body burned, but not as much as his inability to do anything. Evan clenched his fist. "Move on, I can't stand it."

A look flitted across the Overseer's face, but he nodded and continued. His reports were as disengaging as always, but

Evan paid attention this time, as much as he wished he didn't have to.

As soon as Rhys left, Evan would be alone again, so he relished their time they spent together. He had never had friends like others did, even his cousins always had some sort of ulterior motive. Evan wasn't deluded into thinking Rhys liked him for who he was, or that he liked him at all, but as an adviser he had some level of freedom to speak his mind.

Then he was done and rising. Evan tried to get up too, groaning with soreness.

"Please, stay, Your Highness." Rhys motioned him back, then bowed and left.

Evan stretched more, getting some feeling back in his body and massaging some of his muscles to movement again. Now it wasn't a complete burning pain, but a dull constant pain spiked whenever he moved.

He looked to his sword, but couldn't bear the thought of trying another workout. He walked instead, slowly shuffling around his room, then out the door to his study, sword in hand.

The room was as he left it, with plenty of room to word. Drawing the sword was painful, and Evan could barely get through the first form.

He had to stop, and sink into a chair, panting. At least the sun was up.

The room was bathed in a warm glow, the cool stone on his feet felt good. He marveled at how even his toes felt sore and stiff, and stretched them out.

His one candle in the corner, graciously granted by the Overseer's inventory.

It felt good to get off his feet, and he closed his eyes to just listen.

The castle was talking. Somewhere above him wood creaked, a low whistle of wind next to it. Far off in the distance he thought he heard people talking.

It made him long to go out all the more. How could he lead them from in here? And how could he stop a rebellion with no way to reason with his subjects.

He opened his eyes, looking around the room for something, anything that might help him. Furniture, the bar cabinet, his eyes rested on the bookshelf.

Tickles of his former tutors ran through his mind then. One of his first, Archelwaid, had told him books were distilled knowledge, transmuted from age to age.

Could they help him? He doubted it, but there were stranger things that had happened. However, to get there he had to get up first.

He wasn't looking forward to it, but Evan built his resolve, and then finally stood.

Body protesting, he went across the room and stood next to the books, taking in long breaths.

Other memories flooded back to him. Long, boring days listening to old tutors drone on and on, never varying their tone. Hot, warm rooms that made him fall asleep within minutes of the lesson, and sharp raps on the knuckles to wake him up.

It made Evan feel stuffy just to remember, and he hot around his collar. Luckily, it was cold, and that helped to stave off the worst of the thoughts. There was no crackling fire in the hearth, or huge beams of sun to heat this room.

He picked up the one he had taken the other day. It's spine was leather, and aged by time. How long had this book been in his collection, forgotten and lost to time?

Evan turned it over, feeling the embossed letters on the front, and slipped his finger between two pages.

What would Yand think of him, working himself to injury and reading books? Evan smiled, knowing the shocked reaction that would have been visible to only a few that knew the man really well.

Never a scholar himself, Yand knew quite a bit more than he let on. Evan only caught it from others, who had been surprised by Yand's references to popular stories and history, most of it military related.

"Never discount what you can learn from the past. It may save your life one day," Yand had said. Evan grimaced, hard to think of it.

It cracked as he opened it up, all along the spine. He winced, and examined it, but nothing seemed out of place.

Hobbling over to his desk, he took it with him and held it up to his little light coming in the window.

The letters were small, but neatly typed. The first letter was larger and ornamented. Whoever had written this book had taken his time, for vines traveled up the "s" on the first page.

"So follows the history of Chathem from founding to the year of the sun, 9th summer."

He fought the urge to put it down, feeling all his former hatred of letters and words come back in force.

Whoever invented the art could have made things easier. Evan yawned, and settled back in his chair.

He set the book down and tried his arms again, but they were too sore to move.

With nothing else to do, he read. Slowly, at first, with frequent stops, but something about the words caught him, fascinating him.

Soon, he was swept into the history of his people.

14

THE ONE TO LEAVE

The next night was easier for Sam and proved to be more successful. He saw improvement, even in the small amount of work that had come from the workers.

The guardsman, no strangers to fighting and training to fight, had improved as well. Sam stood in the cold, seeing his frosty breath fill the night sky and taken away under the light of the moon.

"I see we were right to trust you," the Overseer said.

Surprised, Sam turned. He couldn't make out the expression in the man's face in the dark, other than he was looking at him.

"Overseer," Sam said, bowing slightly. "I didn't expect to see you out this late."

"I wanted to come and see how everything was going." Overseer Rhys stepped next to him, watching the last session of sparring. Men grunted and struck at each other, practicing the techniques and forms Sam had taught them.

He's out here to observe me. Bill had done everything he said he would so far, and from all that Sam could tell was instrumental in getting his permission to train the men.

"It's a nice night, isn't it?" The Overseer was bundled in clothing, a thick winter coat covering his shoulders and dwin-

106

dling form. "And how does the training go?" He turned to face Sam.

"Well."

"That's all?"

Sam shrugged. "The men are listening and practicing what I tell them. If it were that way with so many others, the world would be a better place."

The Overseer let out a short, bitter laugh. "Perhaps it is on the other side too."

Sam looked to the walls and the Belmarch that lay encamped on the other side of them. "I don't get the feeling that's the case."

"Oh? Go on."

"We haven't seen much action from them."

"I've had reports the enemy still sets up sentries, sends out regular patrols within sight of the walls," the Overseer said.

"All true, but that is a simple matter to attend to, and any leaderless army could do it." Sam shook his head. "They're waiting for something—or some time. I wish I knew what it was."

"Well, in the meantime, you have some work to do." The sparring was wrapping up, and each of the squad leaders was calling an end to the session. "We'll need them well-trained in the event of another breach."

"There was something I wanted to talk to you about that," Sam said, then hesitated.

"Go on," the Overseer said.

"When Yand was here—still alive, I mean." His body had been laid to rest in the makeshift cemetery. "We discussed additional defenses for the castle."

"I remember."

"I think now would be a good time to start. I've noticed the masons don't have much to do and think it would be a better use of their time."

It was a mystery Sam was still trying to unravel. Where was all the effort going? His plans would have taken it all, and then some.

"Yes, I've discussed that with Bill," the Overseer said. Sam shivered as he cooled down, the heat from training wearing off. "I think it would do with some changes, but overall, I'm satisfied."

Everyone was trickling out of the courtyard, putting up their training weapons and returning to the shelter of the Keep. The makeshift shacks now lay abandoned and dark, unusable in the cold.

"I'm glad to hear that," Sam said, thinking carefully about his next words.

"I can see you're thinking about what the drawback is—the price you need to pay." The Overseer stuffed his hands into deep pockets.

"There are some conditions to it. Bill has told me of your plans with the river. That's something I hadn't thought of, and I think it might work."

Sam was glad Bill had some success with the Overseer.

"Come inside, to my room. It's too cold to talk out here," the Overseer said. He turned and walked to the Keep without waiting for Sam to follow.

Sam had to walk fast to catch up but did before they got there. Passing through the door brought a measure of relief from the cold and quieted his shivering muscles.

They didn't say anything else until they were back in the Overseer's office.

After taking a seat at his desk, the Overseer motioned for Sam to join him.

Sam sat, letting his muscles ease into relaxation. His leg throbbing quietly.

The Overseer pressed his fingers together and considered him. A candle gave them light and a tiny measure of warmth, but not much.

"I will be the one to leave."

Sam looked at him, not understanding. "Leave?"

"When you get this boat built, I will be the one to take it for help," the Overseer said.

It took a few moments for the words to sink in. "What do you mean you'll take it? You can't take it."

"I will. I've piloted boats on the water in my youth, and I have the connections. There isn't anyone better to go."

"Who put you up to this? Was it Bill?"

"Bill and I have an understanding." The Overseer's lips tightened.

Sam's heart was racing, wondering why this was happening. *What is Bill planning?*

"What makes you want to go?" he finally asked.

A rueful smile played across the Overseer's lips. "Other than being the one to survive?" he asked. "I don't hide that thought crossed my mind as well, and it is a little perk, assuming its safe to leave in the first place. No, that wasn't it. I want to go because I'm not sure they would listen to anyone else, except perhaps the Duke."

"So, you'll leave him." It wasn't a question, but there was an unspoken one behind it.

"Duke Hornblood has... changed. I know it might leave a precarious position, but what other choice do I have?" The Overseer shrugged and held up his hands. "Who else knows the way to the capital, let alone who can get into the court to bear witness to what happened here?"

Sam knew he couldn't do it and frowned. The long list of people in the castle ran through his mind, but not a single one other than the Duke seemed able to perform that act.

"Then why not send the Duke?" Sam asked.

"It's still a risk. We don't know how well the Belmarch are watching the river, and assuming they are, we all know what will happen to the man in the boat." The Overseer arched his brow. "Assuming it can float, that is."

"It will function as designed," Sam said. He had total confidence in Kerien and Ned, except for that small nagging doubt that lived in the back of his mind. "You said you've done some piloting—what does that mean?"

"It means I know a little something about boats," the Overseer said, smiling. "Don't worry, I can remember it too. I grew up on the river, more than a few miles downriver perhaps, but I'll know my way around when I get there."

"It doesn't seem to be the smartest option," Sam said. "You've been put in charge here."

"Of building a castle fortress. How am I to do that without supplies?" *He has a point.* "With the Duke here, my authority is already lessened. He will pick up the mantle and keep things going."

"How, exactly, will he do that?"

"That's where I need your help. The Duke is young and needs some guidance."

"Guidance? I'm no adviser."

"No, but you do command the respect of everyone in the castle with the way you handled the last attack." The Overseer's eyes glinted in the candlelight. His office smelled of paper and animal skins.

"I can't do it."

"You haven't even heard my proposition yet," the Overseer said.

"I don't need to. I'm not able to be a royal adviser. I can't even really be an adviser on carpentry," Sam said. Each word felt pulled out his body with force, and he felt lightheaded. *What happened to the Overseer Rhys that hated me, that wanted to see me fail and blamed me for everything?*

He couldn't do it. Sam wasn't a general, wasn't even a captain. Now he expected him to be a Duke?

"Perhaps this isn't the best time to discuss it," the Overseer said, his tone softening. "But I will be leaving eventually, so you would do well to think about what life in the castle will look like when that happens."

It didn't feel real. It felt like Sam was in a dream. Like he was enveloped by water. Even the Overseer's voice seemed to be distorted.

He hadn't considered this outcome, not one bit. Sam had wondered if Bill would try and convince the Overseer to send the Duke himself, take care of two in one go. He would be out of the way and one of the best chances to get them help, had he survived the trip downriver.

Never once had he thought the Overseer might want to go, or that it was even an option.

But here it was, staring him in the face.

Sam licked his lips, his mouth suddenly dry. "This is...unexpected is all." he was going to talk to Bill about this one. "We aren't even ready with the boat, let alone the stonework to remove for the crane."

"I can assure you the masons will be ready long before you are." There was the veiled insult. The Overseer kept a blank face as he said it.

"I'm glad of that."

"One less man within the walls means one less mouth to feed," the Overseer said.

It made Sam think about the women and children that were still here, trapped within the walls of the castle. Who was going to get them about? Would word spread about the boat, make it seem like they would be making an escape without them?

Sam's plan suddenly wasn't as good as he originally thought. He grimaced, thinking of Belinda and her child. He imagined lowering them down to get them away, but then something awful happening to the boat and it sinking, taking them down to a watery grave.

He realized then how much of a risk the Overseer was taking, and how much trust he had put within the carpenters of Hornblood Castle. Far more than Sam gave him credit for.

He looked at him in a different light. Gone was the plump of the rich man that had overseen them, gone was the life of ease. He had aged more than Sam had realized, great sunken bags beneath his cheeks accentuated by the candlelight.

The Overseer was a slim man now. *How much was he eating?* Not much more than anyone else, maybe even less.

But there was a strength beneath those eyes, resolve that hadn't been there when they had just been building the castle and not trapped inside. Where had it come from?

Sam swallowed and cleared his throat. "Before I go, we need to discuss something. The defenses."

"Go on," the Overseer said, watching him closely. *What kind of reaction is he expecting?*

"You mentioned changes. What did you want to change?"

The Overseer leaned back and flitted his hand. "Nothing much, a change here and there to make things a little easier on the masons to build."

Sam knew it was too good to be true. Changes to that plan would have neutered its effectiveness. He had seen it happen too. Still, he smiled and tried to be polite. "Can you be more specific?"

"No. Not at this time. If you'd like to know what you'll have to talk to Bill. He knows what he wants." *As I suspected.*

"I understand," Sam said. There was nothing left to discuss, so he stood. "I must be going now, Overseer. It was a pleasure."

"No need to lie Sam. I know this isn't pleasant for anyone, you least of all." He looked off in the distance. "For anyone here."

Sam wondered what the real reason the Overseer wanted to leave was. The attacks had come under his jurisdiction, even though the Duke was here it didn't matter for some reason. The specific reason Sam didn't know, but he knew that it fell to the Overseer to make the castle defensible.

He had failed in that respect, and might be trying to salvage the situation.

Whatever the case, Sam didn't want to spend another minute in the Overseer's office. The scent was getting to him, and it felt stuffy after being outside in the cold so long and so much.

He bid the man goodnight and left. As the door shut with a click behind him Sam knew what he needed to do.

He needed to pay a visit to Bill.

15

RUMBLINGS

Sam wondered when the best time to talk to Bill would be. It was too late that night and too cold outside. The next morning he didn't get a chance, or he didn't feel like it, and even though he saw him at lunch he said nothing to him, only nodded politely and continued on his way.

Bill had changed some, and Sam didn't know if that was a good thing or a bad thing. He didn't think the man had much animosity towards him anymore, but his scheming was even more pronounced now.

"I'm afraid to ask him," Sam said, after he caught Ned alone in the workshop, before the others came back, after he had explained the situation. At least, what he felt comfortable sharing.

"What is the worst that could happen?"

"He wanted too little last time." Sam examined their progressed, feeling the curve in the little bow that was starting to take shape. "I've known Bill long enough to know he asks for more than that." He shook his head. "What is he trying to get out of me?"

"The better question is what is he trying to get for himself?" Ned carved another curl from the wood.

Sam thought about that long and hard, even as the others came in. He made motion for Ned to keep their discussion quiet, which he acknowledged with a nod.

As they ran out of material, they were running out of things to work on. The castle had a good bundle of arrows now, considering they hadn't used any since the last attack they were well stocked.

The iron had run out so they were down to flints and bits of stone that the masons provided, attached by long, thin slivers of bark.

He hadn't been to see Dale in some time, so Sam resolved to go see him. He knew Bill the best of anyone.

Stretching his hands against the cold wasn't helping anymore. The flaps of the workshop did a horrible job of keeping out the wind, no matter how tightly they tied them down, and sucked all heat out of them.

Sam worried about where they would go. There was no warm spot left in the castle, winter had come in full force. Even the snow that was now ankle high offered little relief against it, no matter how high it packed up against the walls of the Keep.

An hour before sunset, came all too early, Sam put up his tools and left the others to their work, checking on the progress. He gave Trent some encouragement, who was helping to prepare the wood for Ned and Kerien, who gave him a small smile in return.

Late-night training sessions wouldn't be possible in a few more days. The wind howled across the courtyard, buffeting him.

His ears stung from little bits of snow that rushed into his face and around his head, and they went into his eyes and made them sting and water. The rivers were kicked up and made a terrible noise. he knew from the last few days they would be raging and foam covered if he went up to see it.

Another thing in the long line of ways to kill their chances. Now they would have to wait for a calm day once the boat was finished to set their expedition to sail.

He was shivering uncontrollability when he stepped into the smithy, which was dark and cold uncharacteristically.

No one was there.

Where could he be? Sam sat near the dark forge, staring at the tooling. Everything was well kept and in its place. Besides a small cobweb here or there it was as if it was waiting in the morning for the forge fires to be lit.

He glanced to the corner. There was some fuel left, a heap of charcoal in its assigned spot. Sam suspected Dale would have another stash, a secret stash, hidden away.

The smell was different. Wrong, somehow. It should be filled with the smell of smoke and burning hot metal, but it was filled with the tasteless bite of winter instead.

"Didn't expect to see you here," Dale said. He came in and stomped his feet. "No one comes around."

"How much fuel do you have left?" Sam asked.

"A few days, maybe a week, if I keep the fire going." He sat down next to Sam, pulling up a stool. It wobbled. "I've been meaning to ask you to fix that. Hadn't had much time to sit on it though."

"All it seems you have is time," Sam said.

"Ha," Dale said. "I haven't seen you much, just at training. I see you're leading it now." He looked at him through the corner of his eye.

"They asked me to." Sam shrugged.

"That's not the Sam Freeman I knew." It was warmer in the smithy than outside, shielded from the wind, but only just. Still, Sam wanted to talk alone, to figure things out together.

"A lot has changed. I realized there are people here I care about, that need a chance."

Dale nodded. "We could all use some of that. There is a fragileness in the air, Sam. I know you feel it too."

He did and didn't want to think about it. "I need your opinion on Bill."

"I wouldn't trust him with a hammer or tongs. You avoided the question."

"You didn't ask a question."

"Fine. Can you feel it too?"

Sam paused. "I feel it. Anarchy, rebellion, that's what I feel. All at the wrong time." He shook his head. "We shouldn't be fighting among ourselves."

"Not everyone sees it that way."

"Then how do they see it?"

It was Dale's turn to pause. "Some see it as casting off the old, so that we have a chance to survive. I've even heard talk of surrender to the Belmarch from some of the younger ones."

"Surrender? Would they accept it."

"They'd accept it all right, then come in a kill us anyway and take the women back to Belmarch as slaves and playthings." Sam bristled at the thought of it, at Belinda being abused.

And Martha.

It touched something strange within him to think about. *Why did I think of her?*

"They'd be fools to do it, but desperate men are foolish creatures."

"And that's what I've come to talk to you about." Sam filled him in. "I know we need the masons to put up any real defenses. Stone is the only thing we have plenty of, but how do I trust a man not worthy of it?"

"You can't, can you." Dale leaned back on his stool, resting his back against a bench. "I'm not sure you have much of a choice though. You think these defenses would work?"

"I do."

"And you're willing to risk all our lives on them?" Dale's eyes bored in to his.

"I don't think I'd be doing that. We have the walls, we have the gate. I just don't think they'll stand."

"What if they don't come in that way, that they break through somewhere else?"

"I've thought about that," Sam said. "Every time I keep coming back to that weak spot. It's too good to pass up. The walls are too thick and they know it."

"How do you know?"

"Because if they thought they could break into the walls they would be bombarding us every day with that catapult."

"But they aren't."

Sam nodded. The sky was changing color already, the sunset already coming on. "They haven't yet, and I don't think they will unless someone else is in charge." It made sense to him, but this was the first time he had voiced it out loud. "They are going to starve us, Dale. And I think they'll succeed."

They were silent as the wind ran through the workshop roof, howling and screaming as it went. No children played outside now. the stool creaked as Dale shifted his eight.

"What did you come to me for?"

"I need to know what you think Bill is after."

"After?" Dale's eyes widened a hair, and he scratched his beard. "Seems to me that Bill is after what most men are after. Power."

"That's what I thought too, but then why wouldn't he take it earlier? Why would he ask me to lead a revolt?"

"In hopes that you fail, or better yet, that you succeed. He's probably thought about both outcomes and how he might use either to his advantage," Dale said. "Be careful of him, he's smarter than he lets on."

"I know, and I've felt some of it already." Sam thought back to the Overseer and conversations he had with him. "Have you... sensed any change within Bill?"

Dale frowned. "Changed? No, I think he's still the same man he always was. Why do you ask?"

"Hes' talking to me, for one thing," Sam said. "Something he said to me, a conversation we had. I don't know, maybe I'm giving him too much credit."

"You might be. But, then again, you might be right. A lot has changed. Almost everything. You can expect men to stay the same after that, even if they seem like they are. You're a good example."

"I don't see it that way."

"And you don't have to, but you know it to be true anyway." The sky was orange now, big clouds racing across the sky. Hints of red were starting to show. "Either way, you have to decide if this course of action is something you believe in enough to take the risk."

Risk. He wondered what kind of risk it would be. To be in the service of a man he hardly trusted, but had something inside that made him hope for the best.

And it could all be for naught. He could put himself in Bill's hands only to be wrenched and betrayed, cast aside like some little used piece of cloth, or moldy food.

"I don't know what to do."

"You'll have to figure that out soon." Dale nodded and looked out the door. Bill was walking across the courtyard, flanked by masons. It was like he was a king holding court, the way they simpered and deferred to him.

Sam burned with anger, and more than a hint of jealousy. Perhaps he had run from his old life for more reasons than he was convincing himself of. There was a yearning desire inside him to be loved and respected.

But he expected that Bill has the Sam desire, as did all of them. The thought gave him pause, made him consider the choice before him n another light.

"Thank you. You've given me something to think about," Sam said, standing and taking Dale's hand. He knew his hands were cold, he never expected Dale's to be. Not after working in the smithy for so long, the man was always warm.

"Whatever you do, make sure you know it's the right thing." Dale's eyes burned into his, a deep fire raging within him. His hand throbbed with strength. Sam was sure he could crush his hand in an instant.

For all the times he had seen Dale work, he had never seen him angry. And, to think of it, he had never seen him fight.

Right then, though, he was glad Dale was on his side.

"Can I count on your friendship and support?"

"I might want to call it a favor," Dale said, his eyes twinkling and creases of happiness appearing around his eyes. It was the first time Sam had seen him happy in a while.

It was the first time he had seen anyone happy in a while. Imagine that.

He longed for the old days, the simple days of sweat and toil, a hard, hot, long day that had a feast at the end of it and a great, big bonfire where the workers and their families could gather and talk and laugh and sing.

There was none of that here. Even if they were warm enough, they were too hungry. Even if they were fed, they would despair. He saw it every time he went into the keep.

They might lose more of them to hopelessness than anything else.

"I'll take what I can get. You won't have much use of a favor from me if I'm dead." *Not that I want to die.*

"Then you best keep yourself alive." Dale rubbed his hands together. "Back out into the cold again."

Sam nodded. "Back out once more." He started first, leaving the cold smithy to sit undisturbed.

"Where are you going?" Dale asked.

Sam looked over his shoulder, face set in a grim mask. "To make my decision."

16

HISTORY OF CHATHEM

Evan read the book. In it he discovered things he had never known and remembered hard lessons his tutors had tried to teach him long ago.

It took him back to days by the river, an exercise his father frowned upon, listening to Master Raupth drone on about the early history of the Chathem tribe.

He had soaked in the sunshine those days, and retained little of his lessons, but those lessons started to come back to him now.

It took a different light, when he was finally able to put away the hard words and work through the letters. As he went, he discovered more.

The story of Adol and the Snake, how he had tricked the pour beast into blessing his future line, thus beginning the tribe of Chathem.

The guile, the cunning it took to convince the snake to come out of his hole, the bravery to grab it by the throat despite the fangs dripping venom, Evan wondered why he had never heard these stories before.

But, as he thought about it, he realized he may have. Evan, as bad as he was with studies and books, had tried to avoid them as a child.

Now, he realized that within the pages of these tomes he could find something else. Something of his descendants, those who had gone before him.

He flipped through the pages, learning and absorbing more and more. The crease of the spine, the smell of the leather and animal skin, it took him to another world.

Shimmering on the page, the deep black ink invited him in in stark contrast to the dull gray of the stone that surrounded him. At each new story there was a small illustration around the first letter, drawn with great care and related to the history that followed.

He started to look forward to these new pages, even the long chronologies that punctuated some of the book that bored him.

A knock on his door announced the arrival of lunch. Evan looked up, surprised that it was already that late in the day.

He set the book down and stood, glad that some of his soreness had abated. He used the opportunity to walk around and stretch out his muscles some more as the servant set his food on the table.

He was a young man, dark eyed and dark hair. Evan had seen him before, recognized the face, but realized he didn't even know his name.

"Good afternoon, Your Highness," the man said, bowing to leave.

"Wait, what is your name?" Evan tried to suppress the feeling of annoyance as a flicker of fear went across the man's face.

"It does not matter, Your Highness." He wouldn't look Evan in the eye, but he couldn't blame him for that.

"Nonsense, I asked you a question and I demand an answer." He was used to having better conversation, and thought as he said it he might have been missing the sound of another human's voice.

It was tiring to listen to Rhys for an hour or two and then spend the rest of your day in solitude.

"Barger, Your Highness," he said, mumbling it quietly.

"Barger?" The man's lips tightened. "A...solid name, for a solid man. How long have you been a s-" Evan hastily changed his question, "with us?"

"A year, your highness."

A year? There was no way that was true. Evan though back, realizing with a sickening feeling that the man was telling the truth. He had come with him in the spring, and had served him the summer before that. Evan remembered him being at the harvest festival.

His cheeks reddened, also remembering the amount of wine he had consumed that night.

"Yes, good to have you too." Evan smiled, the smile he used when he didn't feel like it but was told to anyway. Silence stretched between them.

"Shall I leave you to dine, your highness?" Barger asked.

"Oh, yes." The man turned and opened the door. "Thank you," Evan said as he walked out, trying to overcome his previous ineptitude.

The man stopped mid-stride, then continued on, shutting the door without even a click.

That made him remember even more. Barger was his silent servant, always sneaking up on him. You could never hear him coming.

Evan took another lap around his room, glancing at the tray. Served on the best dishes the castle had to offer, it was still going to be a tasteless gruel of mashed up wheat.

He took off the metal cover, fearing he was right. Evan sighed and sat down to eat.

It was as he feared, and each bite had to be chewed what seemed like forever before he could finally choke it down.

But he needed the sustenance after yesterday. After he finished he pushed away the dishes in disgust and found he felt better.

Wine would make the bland taste out of my mouth. Evan glanced to the cupboard. All he had to do was summon his servant and Rhys and send them to get the second to last cask. It would be a relief.

And it would bring oblivion.

Evan stared at it until he couldn't look at it anymore. He ripped himself away from it and practically lunged at his sword, drawing it in a flash.

The sword rang out, caught by the edge of the scabbard. He immediately went into his first form, letting it flow through him.

He thought about little as he did, a momentary question of how many times he had done this floating to the top of his consciousness, then swept away into the forms.

His body was looser than when he started. It still was sore, but not as severe. Evan continued on, working on the next forms in series.

Each one was more advanced than the last, adding more motions and techniques with every step. Eventually he finished them all.

Sweating, he stopped to catch his breath. Panting, he realized that if he kept going he would end up worse off tomorrow. Reluctantly, he sheathed his sword and took it off, setting it carefully over the edge of the table.

He went back to the book. Later, he wasn't sure if it was a few hours or a few minutes, Barger knocked again and came in to take his plates.

Evan said nothing to him except "Thank you" as he left. Barger bowed with politeness, but said nothing in return.

Evan was surprised he spoke the first time. He returned to his studies, poring over the book.

There were more interesting stories the more he read.

Belthaz and his double hammers, making the enemies flee before him in battle. Shiraf the Thief who managed to bring an army to its knees planting treasures within it.

But it was Miral that captured his imagination and attention. There, in the dark light of the room, he stumbled upon a story he had never heard of.

A son of Yuoled the Bold, Miral had been a disappointment to his father in his youth, so much so that he was passed over to inherit the kingdom of Chathem in favor of his uncle.

Before his father's death, Miral tried to entreat with him to earn back his inheritance. Yuoled refused, and within a few hours had breathed his last.

Before the coronation of his uncle, they were attacked by Belmarch armies from the north. Each page revealed more and more desperation the kingdom faced as a power vacuum emerged.

The coronation was put on hold, the nobles tried to raise their armies. Each one fought against another, vying for the kingship.

All the while the Belmarch army marched south, burning and looting as they went. Lacastia fell, then Mayfield. His uncle tried to unite then under one banner, but only succeeded in taking half the kingdom's forces to Antilia and a final defense.

All the while Miral was helpless in the capitol, then Gold-ever. He had taken to drink, and was ridiculed by all.

But the news of his uncles death at Antilia roused him from his stupor. Miral swore off all drink and shaved his head in mourning. There was no clear successor, and he was not sure the nobles would accept him.

They didn't, at first. Miral enlisted the aid of his mother, the Queen Soleth, and began to turn them one by one to his cause.

The Belmarch, not desiring anything other than complete domination and the resources of Chathem, pushed forward into the very heart of Chathem.

Miral was told of a weakness, their supplies and baggage train that trailed all the way north to Belmarch. He took his much smaller army and headed north, proclaiming his intent to fight on the field of battle and earn his father's crown.

The light faded as he read, and he had to pause to light a candle. The small flame danced and tricked its way around the wick, filling the room with the aroma of smoke.

Soreness had set back into his muscles, and he worked them loose again before he returned to his book. Dinner came while he did, and he wolfed it down and returned to the book, marveling at how much he looked forward to it.

Miral traveled north, but not to meet them in battle. He turned east, and using old roads and trails unknown to the Belmarch, circled around them with forced marches.

All the while he kept his head bald and trained harder than he ever had. Master swordsmen taught him everything they knew, and he quickly became a deadly fighter.

When they reached the back lines of the Belmarch they stood unopposed. Miral freed prisoners and took weapons and arms, and cut off their supplies.

The Belmarch were not dissuaded, and kept their troops fed from the ravaging of the lands. But, winter was nearly upon them, and the Belmarch didn't plan for a cold weather encounter.

Miral had, and he had grown his ranks with prisoners and converts alike. He made promises to the nobles, and increased his strength. Dukedoms were established, and with a thrill Evan realized that a minor noble was granted the Hornblood line in that very story.

He continued reading. Miral trapped the Belmarch in the low country, defeating them in a climatic battle that clinched his title to the throne and established his right to rule. The few Belmarch that survived fled north, around his army, and barely any survived. He established peace in his time and became a great rule, enacting justice fairly and impartially and growing his kingdom. Lands to the east and west joined, establishing the boundaries up to the Golden River.

Evan sat back, the end of the tail finished, and basked in the glow of the candlelight. By all accounts Miral was a failure that had risen above his previous failures to become something better.

The candle flickered. It was late now, and his eyes were heavy. His body would recover with rest, but his mind was on fire and alight with what he had read.

It could be possible.

He went back through the chapter, making sure he hadn't read it wrong. He didn't.

Why had no one told me this before? Did they even know? The books on his bookshelf were little used, but varied. What else lay within their covers?

Evan wanted to read more. It was a strange sensation, and one he had never expected to feel. he got up and paced around the room, both to stretch his legs and clear his mind.

Thoughts ran through him, flying past one another at an astounding speed. He thought about what he could do from these rooms, how he might have lost a chance before but might have another one.

But was it too late? Evan chewed on his lip and stretched his arms. they too were still sore, even more so than his legs.

He couldn't sort it all out though, and his candle was getting too low. It smelled less like smoke and more like tallow, and Evan took it with him to his bedroom.

There was no one in the hall, and his footsteps echoed. The door creaked as it opened and shut behind him.

Evan dressed for bed, staring hard at himself in the water of his washbasin. He looked different than he had, and wasn't sure why.

From somewhere far outside his room he heard an owl hoot. A good omen, this far into winter. It meant that good weather would come, and that the winter would be short.

Evan watched a smile grow on his face. Things might be the same tomorrow, or they might be different. Evan suspected they would be different.

17

BITING COLD

Sam stood in the freezing cold, barely able to handle it. His entire body was shaking with shivers.

There was nothing happening, and he wished he could be inside, away from the cold blowing win that cut right through him to the heart. The sun was obscured by a thick layer of gray clouds.

He checked the southern horizon, not seeing any movement, and looked back into the castle and the courtyard.

No one was out. Everyone not on watch on the walls was tucked inside, away from the wind and blowing snow. They had made a path through the drifts, from the keep to the stairs coated in ice up to the battlements.

The Keep looked pitiful. It was squat and coated in snow, icicles hanging from beams and roofs. It should have had tall towers and another floor.

Sam lamented this. Had they been able to continue their work the next floor would have been on by now, and the southwest tower would have been driven into the sky.

He imagined knocking home the final beam, standing astride it and looking into the wilderness beyond. He would have been able to see into Belmarch clearly, and far upriver.

Instead, it was a shell of its former self. And he was no closer to finishing it. He supposed he should be grateful, that he was still alive when others had perished, but strangely enough he wasn't.

Hie was deeply unsatisfied. So much so he couldn't look at it anymore and turned back to the village below.

Sam gripped his bow tight, hoping to squeeze some amount of warmth from it. They were doing hour long watches now, it was too cold for anything longer.

He didn't know what time of year it was, but he knew they had reached the coldest and bitterest part of winter. Hardly any sun light up the days now, and when it was clouds covered over most their light.

It started to snow a few moments later. a rough, biting snow that stung his cheeks and made his eyes water.

A man came up to relieve him. He couldn't tell who it was, his face was covered in threadbare cloth.

Sam turned over his bow and arrows, hands thick with cold, and went back into the warmth of the guardhouse.

They had half the number of sentries on the wall then usual, partly because of the cold and partly because there was no way an attack would have been successful in those conditions.

Inside, men were shivering and huddled together to keep warm. Sam joined them, pressing into the mass.

"Bitter cold out there," he said. The door swung open and shut, letting in a blast that set him shivering.

"It won't let up," Mathew said. His ears were an unnatural red color. He rubbed his shoulders and joined the rest of them.

There was little conversation as the newcomers tried to get warm again. Sam longed for a thick, fur coat to wrap himself in. They had scarcely any more clothes to protect themselves from the cold, and it was starting to take its toll.

A man had died out there, young and in his prime. His name had been Nathula, and he was a mason. Bill had stumbled upon him when he went to his watch, frozen up on the wall.

He had been blue and stuck to the rock. It had taken hours to thaw him out enough to get his clothes off, and they put him outside in the shelter of the Keep. The ground was too hard to try and dig up, but his body would stay preserved.

It was one more life lost, one more death. The specter of it hung over the survivors, and that had made them shift to shorter watches. It had been Mathew's idea, and a good one.

"One of the worst winter's I've seen," a man said, from back in the group. "We've been cursed. We'll never make it through the winter."

"We've made it this far," Sam said, finally getting a hold of his chattering teeth enough to speak. "We'll make it."

But he wasn't sure. It was bitter cold, much worse than last year. He hoped his words didn't sound hollow, but couldn't be sure.

In no time at all their respite was up, and the next group of sentries pushed out into the cold to take their turn. The group shifted around and pressed together, and Sam found himself closer to the center.

A few minutes later the relieved sentries came in, stamping and puffing, and joined them. It went on like this all through their watch, until the light was gone and th next squad had their turn.

Sam joined the others in turning over the equipment, and wondered how far Ned and Kerien had gotten. If they didn't finish soon they wouldn't have a chance of getting that boat launched.

The winter storms had driven the rivers into a frenzy. How they were going to a get a boat to float on it, he didn't know, but they couldn't wait for better weather. Every day brought them one step closer to starving.

They fought across the courtyard through the driving snow, and into the Keep in a mass. Dinner was served, a cold mush of unidentified grains, that barely filled their stomachs.

Martha was there, scooping out their portions. Sam's heart skipped a beat when she looked at him and then quickly looked away.

Sam greeted her when it was his turn, and held out his bowl.

"Thank you," he murmured, shivers still racking his body. Her hands were cold as he took the bowl from her.

"How bad is it out there?" Worry creased the corners of her eyes.

"Bad," he said, shoving the mush around his bowl with a spoon. How long he could stand it, he didn't know. They tried their best, but the cooks had nothing to work with. Just stores of grain. "I'm afraid the ice might take someone over the side."

How long would any of them last, with things how they were now? Martha seemed to sense his discomfort.

"You don't bear the weight of the world on your shoulders," she said softly, tenderly.

Sam looked away from her. He couldn't take the look in her eyes. It was... too much to bear.

"I have enough of it to last me a lifetime." He lingered in line, as the last man there was no one behind him.

All of a sudden he was starting to get warm. His mind had wandered, thinking of if Martha was available to eat with him. It seemed absurd, against the backdrop of everything else that was going on.

"Don't be too hard on yourself," Martha said. She turned back. "Girls, go eat."

"Have you ... eaten?" Sam asked. He didn't know why his mouth felt like cotton all of a sudden, or why his palms went sweaty.

When was the last time he had thought about a woman this way? It had been months, years perhaps. Not that he didn't mind admiring some of the better-looking women around, but they were all taken and married.

Belinda. His mind raced to her without thinking. Not all of them were taken now. Far too many widows had been made already, and he hoped there would be none more.

But he knew that was a vain hope.

Martha was staring at him. "I haven't eaten yet." There was a long pause, and Sam shuffled.

If his food was warm, it would have grown cold. He didn't know what to do. He wanted to talk more to Martha but couldn't invite himself to invite her to eat with him.

No matter how hard he tried, and how he opened his mouth, the words didn't seem to leave his lips. It was like they were stuck at the back of his mouth, clogged and caught in his throat.

"If you don't shut your mouth, you'll look like a fish," Martha said, her lips flattening.

Sam's eyes opened wide. "W-What?" he stammered.

The other girls were being dished up. Martha plopped a portion into bowls and passed them out. When the group had come through, he found himself alone with her.

His eyes cast around the room. He found there were many staring at him, and he balked.

"Are you going to eat, Mr. Freeman?" Martha asked, folding her arms with a spoon. Her eyes twinkled with mirth.

"I'm not a—" Sam stopped, realizing she was joking. "Oh." Finally, he rushed the words out, trying not to think of them. "Would you care to sit with me?"

Martha lowered her head and looked out from under her eyelashes at him. "I'd be delighted."

His stomach turned somersaults, despite how empty it was. Even though it wouldn't be filled, he felt a small thrill of giddiness.

They walked to an open spot on a rickety bench, and Sam let her sit down before he took his seat. It was cold in the great hall, but having her next to him felt good. It was as if she warmed the air around herself.

They ate in silence for a while, a strange feeling lingering in the air. He noticed her long, brown hair was unkempt but had a luster of beauty. She had been plump, but like so many others, had lost weight.

Now she looked too thin, and it pained him to see the loss of life in her cheeks. That was one thing he remembered from before the siege. She'd had such rosy cheeks when she was happy.

"Have you been working on anything?" she asked.

"Yes. No, I mean." Why was he all twisted up in knots? He hadn't been like this since he was a child. "I have the others working on a boat."

"A boat?" She turned to him, surprised. "Why on the green earth are you building that?"

"I hope to use it to get help," he mumbled, all of a sudden feeling very foolish. It seemed like the better plan was to wait, but when he explained it to her, she nodded.

"That's a sensible plan, a right fine one. Do put what I said before out of your mind."

"I wish I could do more." Sam stirred the little remaining gruel around in his bowl. He thought he might be able to use it to hold up the castle if he waited long enough; it was so thick. "I can't sleep much at night."

"The cold bothers me too," Martha said.

"No, it isn't that. Not just that, at least." He looked up through the small opening that served as a window at the top of the ceiling. It let in the cold, but it let in light too.

"What is it?" Martha's voice was soft and warm, barely a whisper.

"What am I supposed to do for Belinda and her child? It tears me up inside to see them ... like they are."

"Do you not feel like you're doing enough?"

"No." He shook his head. There wasn't much other conversation, barely a hushed whisper here and there. His voice was lost in the cavernous room. "She deserves better than what she has." He turned to her, earnestly looking in her eyes. "So do you. All of you."

"We did know what we were getting into."

"But she didn't deserve to lose her husband." As soon as he said it, he knew it was a mistake. "I-I didn't mean..."

"No, it's fine." She wiped her eye with her hand. All of Sam's hope drained away from him then, seeing her in such a state of sadness. There was a clatter from the makeshift kitchen. "I have to go now, can't let the girls get away with not doing their fair share."

Martha stood and lifted her chin. Sam knew he should say something to her to make it right but didn't know what it would be.

Once again, he had made a mistake that he couldn't recover from. Another, in a long line and a long list. She marched away, head held high.

It must still be fresh for her, a wound that hadn't healed. Her husband had been dead for some months now, but he had just wanted to talk to her about Belinda. He never meant for it to come to this.

He watched her go, helpless

18

BOTTLES

The next day was easier for Evan. His body was less sore, and he had started to recover. He only groaned a few times getting out of bed. Most days he was woken by breakfast, or they waited until he was awake to bring him his food. That morning he was up long before breakfast, and had enough time to stretch and massage his muscles.

Cold and damp had set into his room, and he shivered as he ate the tasteless meal. Rhys had advised him not to use too much of the candle at once, so he ate in the dark, barely able to see.

When he was finished Evan pushed his meal away. He thought about going through the door that went directly into his office, but then looked at the door to the corridor.

Indignation rose inside him, and anger. He should be able to go out there, to walk among his people without fear. They were his subjects.

But, then again, are they? His father had always said he needed to earn his place, earn the respect of his people. It was one of the most infuriating comments that Evan had to endure, but then again he wondered if there wasn't some wisdom to those words.

"Finished, Your Highness?" Barger was at his elbow, and Evan jumped a little.

"I didn't see you there. Yes, I'm done." The door was open, but he didn't remember hearing it.

"Apologies, I didn't mean to frighten you, Your Highness." Barger took the dishes away with a grace and efficiency Evan couldn't help but admire. The man was quiet, almost too quiet.

"Have you eaten already?" Evan asked.

"Yes, Your Highness." Barger walked to the door, and turned. "Is that all?"

"Yes, that is all." Barger gave a small bow, then left. The door creaked shut, but barely clicked.

Evan dressed, then went into his study. he spent the first part of the morning running through his form work, until he had a light sweat running and dispelled some of the cold.

After that he refreshed himself with water, almost ice cold from sitting out all night, but it felt good on his throat. It consolidated in a lump in his stomach, a strange sensation.

He was glad they had dug the well last summer. From what Rhys had said they weren't going to do it, but it was more convenient for the workers to be able to use the water for their mortar rather than lugging ti up from the river. Of that, Evan wasn't sure, but he was glad that they weren't running out of water like they were everything else.

He still had some time before lunch, so after a few laps around his study, it was light enough to read.

Before he returned to his histories he perused the bookshelf once again. It had twenty, maybe thirty books on it, a small fortune. Evan had wanted to leave them behind, lighten the load of his luggage, but his mother had insisted.

Thinking of her brought a pang of sadness. He wished he could see her now, talk to her. His mother always had good counsel.

And she would know what to do in this kind of situation. She had spent her whole life in the land of courtiers and counsels, a daughter of the neighboring Dukedom of Haverville.

Evan tapped the spine of a book, then pulled it out. She had selected these for him, perhaps there was something within their pages that she was trying to tell him.

On a whim he swept up three or four random books and took them to his desk.

He laid them out in a square, the histories off to the side. There was a brown one, a light blue, and two darker brown books. He picked the one with the most cracks on its cover and opened it.

Its pages were yellowed with time. They gave off a strange smell, one he couldn't describe, and he had to be careful of them because they felt so fragile. Each time he picked up a leaf he held his breath, then turned it.

His eyes narrowed as he read the title. Boat Building? *What reason would I ever have to build a boat?*

There it was though, in black in that was faded around the edges. *Boat-building on the Venti; Historical Accounts of the Drydocks.*

Evan put aside his trepidation for a moment and dove into the reading. It might not be as boring as he thought.

But, that turned out to be a fear realized. It was so boring he found himself nodding off within a few paragraphs of the detailed account of shipbuilding drydocks and the years they were established.

He shook his head and shut the book. Why would anyone even consider writing this book, let alone reading it? It was a waste of paper and ink, as far as he was concerned.

He set it off to the side, then leafed through the other books, getting up to get the rest of them off the bookshelf.

A few minutes later he had them separated into two different stacks, one stack had a glimmer of something that might be interesting. Books on war tactics, fighting, and history.

The other stack he wasn't sure what he was going to do with. They had books on industry, mathematics, and architecture. Each one almost put him to sleep within seconds of reading through them. the one on architecture made his eyes glaze over just at the title alone.

Barger brought in his lunch then, after knocking. This time he heard it.

Evan looked at the space on his desk taken up by books, and the table covered with his sword and belt set there after his form work.

Barger also looked from one to the other, holding the tray carrying his food. There was nowhere to set it down.

He watched the servant in his conundrum, then Evan was finally compelled to stand and do something about it.

He picked up his sword, setting it on his desk among the books. The crest of the Hornbloods loomed up above him.

"Anything else, Your Highness?" Barger asked. He glanced tot he books as he stood straight.

"Can you read?" Evan asked.

"A little. Not much."

"Be glad of that. I've been looking through them all morning and might need to take a nap now." Evan smiled, hoping to see something of a rise from his servant.

But, he hoped in vain. Barger's expression never changed, and he didn't say anything.

Evan's smile faded. The hatred he heard about had spread even to his own servants.

But as he thought about how he had treated them, how he didn't even acknowledge their existence, he started to realize why.

"Would you fill up the bottles and bring them back." Barger stared at him. "Please?" Evan said through grounding teeth.

I shouldn't have to beg for what is mine.

"I was...advised against it, Your Highness."

Evan's face flushed. His anger grew. "By whom?"

Barger shifted from foot to foot, and then looked down at the ground.

"Fine, don't tell me. I already know who. You will brig me the wine, however. I still hold some sway in this castle." A simple letter would take care of all of this, if he could only get it delivered.

How had his mother handled their servants? He tried to think back, to remember the interactions between them. He had heard she held a particularly strong sway over them from others, but hadn't the foggiest clue why. Nor did he care enough to find out.

He supposed she treated the same as everyone else, with a light touch and a large amount of care. Always coming in behind his father, as strong as iron, to clear things up and smooth over hurt feelings.

"As you wish, your highness. How many should I fill?"

"Three." That would be enough to last him through the night. His throat was parched anyway, the reminder of it making him thirsty. "Make it four."

Barger crossed the room again, after a quick bow, swept up four bottles in his hand, and was gone a few seconds later.

Evan cursed himself inside, and paced around the room. His anger subsided, and he realized that he made a mistake.

It was easier to avoid the drink if he didn't have any around him. Evan chewed on his lip. *What would it be like to have more than he needed within arm's reach?*

He wished Barger had told him no more forcefully, that Rhys had taken it and gotten rid of the wine. He wished he had the strength to put it away.

He wasn't sure he could resist it, but he wanted it. To loosen his body and mind, to escape the thoughts that ran through his mind.

To ease the pressure that fell upon his shoulders.

Once again he wondered what it was like to be a commoner, to not have the burden he carried. There were no late-night conversations with Yand to be had now.

Evan had to face it. He was on his own now. No father, no mother, no advisers to guide him on his way through the twisted wood of life.

He heard Barger coming this time, the tinkling of bottles proceeded him. Evan paced, waiting for the inevitable, the danger he had asked for brought into this room.

Without a word, Barger entered and knelt by the small cabinet that held his bottles and goblets.

One. Two. Three. Four. Each bottle set down quietly, all in a neat row. Four, just as he had asked.

Evan stared at them. They were filled with dark, red wine, still moving as they settled into place. His body screamed at him to take it in, to drink it.

His mind screamed at him to order Barger to take them away, pour them out, destroy them. His mouth dried up, and he took a shaking breath.

Barger was staring at him, expectantly. Evan's eyes flicked from him to the wine and back again, and smiled nervously.

What did he have to prove to his own servants? Evan pulled back his shoulders and stuck out his chin, then walked over to the cabinet and poured himself a goblet of wine.

It splashed with a tinkling, happy laugh into the goblet, inviting him to drink it in a long pull.

He saw his reflection in the surface of the wine, dark as night. Eyes that were hollow and drawn. *Is that was I look like now?*

It wasn't good to drink alone, that lesson he remembered from long ago. Those that did so had a problem.

But there was no one to drink with, except Barger. Rhys wouldn't be in for another hour, and the glass was poured.

"Would you care for some?" Evan thrust the goblet to Barger.

Shock was an understatement for the expression that came across the servants face.

"It wouldn't be proper, Your Highness."

"I've drunk with commoners many a time before. Besides, I have no need of any, and you look like you could use some fortification." Barger touched his cheek, which was thin from lack of food. "Come, joint me at my table. You don't have anything better to do, do you?"

Evan sat down, and pulled out a chair for Barger to sit in.

"I-"

"Don't make me give you an order. It wouldn't feel right."

Barger, who looked like a hapless deer caught in a trap, took a seat and the offered goblet. His mother might have her way of keeping her servants happy, perhaps he could come up with his own way.

"You look uncomfortable, why not sit back?" Evan asked.

Barger looked like he tried to relax, putting a stiff back up against the chair. the smell of wine drifted out of his goblet. Evan wanted to take a sip so badly, but hid it with a smile.

"Go on, I'll have mine later." Evan watched as Barger lifted the goblet to his mouth, sniffed it, licked his lips, and finally took a sip.

Evan felt somewhat of a thrill, as something forbidden always tastes sweet. But, just as the feeling never lasts, it turned bittersweet as he noticed the expression on Barger's face. He liked the wine, perhaps too much.

Like a rush of water, Evan's own desire to drink welled up inside. He gripped the edge of his chair, but he wasn't sure he could hold back from the temptation.

Evan looked over to the wine, mouth watering.

19

DREAMS AND FIRE

Evan stared at the wine, feeling the crushing weight of wanting. *This was* a *mistake, yet again.* Barger was being polite, taking small sips of wine, but Evan could tell he wanted to drain the glass in one go. He didn't blame him, either.

"How was it you came into my service?" Evan asked.

Barger paused drinking, and set down the goblet. Streaks of wine ran down the rim back into the goblet. The smell was so overwhelming that Evan couldn't take it. He listened to try and keep himself preoccupied.

"I've been serving the Hornbloods since I was a child. My father and mother served the Duke. Naturally, it fell to me to continue the family business." Some of his stiffness had gone. The wine was fortifying him.

"And you came with us on the journey north?"

"Naturally."

Evan didn't remember Barger coming with them, but there had been a long train of people and carts that accompanied him—supplies for the castle, for the most part. Men were part of that, supplied for labor and garrison.

"I would have preferred to stay in Hornblood Hall, but..." Barger dropped his gaze as he trailed off.

"I understand. I didn't want to leave, either." Evan's fingers itched to hold the goblet, to feel the coolness. He felt the pommel of his sword instead. "Did your father force you to go?"

"No. Not my father."

"I see we have something in common, then. Did you leave behind a sweetheart or a wife?"

Barger shook his head, each movement precise and only as large as it needed to be. The man seemed to be restrained in everything. "No wife. There was... a girl."

"Ah." Evan winked at him and tapped the side of his nose. "Say no more, as long as she wasn't too much money."

Barger turned white, then the color rushed to his cheeks as he realized what Evan meant.

"I-I must be going. I have a lot to do." He stood up, nearly knocking over the chair behind him.

"I meant no insult by it."

"No, it isn't that. I'm sorry, I shouldn't have stepped out of my duties."

"At least finish your wine."

"Excuse me, Your Highness." Barger was strait as an arrow again, back stiff as a tree trunk. "I must attend to my duties."

"Very well." Evan waved a hand, and like that, Barger was gone, leaving him in silence. Alone.

It was all he was ever going to be.

Evan stood and walked over to the goblet. It was mostly gone, a few small drops at the bottom. It would be so easy.

But he knew he shouldn't. He knew what would come of it. The pounding head, the feeling in the morning after.

He swept the sword out of its scabbard and into the first form. He fed everything into that form, his desire, his frustration, his longing.

When he was finished, he moved into the next form. Then the next. Then the next.

By the time he had finished them all, he was feeling better, although he was covered in sweat and breathing heavily. Enough time had passed that he felt little need to take the wine now.

Instead of continuing his practice, focusing on adjusting each technique until it flowed well and right into the next one, he slid his sword back into its scabbard with a click.

It was darker now, and it looked like it was snowing heavily, so he lit a candle and went back to his desk and the books piled on it.

He flipped through a book on military tactics. It was dry, running through battles in an ordered and academic way. All the fun had been sucked out of it, but he kept reading.

He had to go over some of the sentences a few times, they were so difficult to understand, but he started to get the hang of it. He even started enjoying the reading, when it wasn't too boring.

His heart skipped a beat when he came to a chapter on sieges. He devoured the whole chapter in one go, not stopping to reread anything.

It set out the reasons for sieging, and tactics to do so, then went to the defending side on how to break them. Preparation seemed to be the biggest factor of success, according to the author.

"Set up large stores of food, fuel, and timber. Segregate each by type, and keep it free from damp and pest. Rationing is vital to the preservation and success of a siege."

So far, everything he had read seemed straightforward, but none of it was particularly helpful.

His heart was beating fast when he came to the end of the chapter. He read it again, to be sure. When he was done, he set the book down and tried to think about how he could use what he'd read.

They couldn't break out—not with fewer defenders in the castle than attackers outside—without suffering major casualties.

Rhys would be here soon to update him on the inventory. Evan sat up in his chair, remembering the report from yesterday. They were running out of everything. They weren't ready for a siege, but one had come anyway.

And now he realized the Belmarch intended to wait them out, not waste lives on attacking when they could expect the Chathem defenders to give up or starve to the point they would offer no resistance.

And then they would kill them. One by one or all at once through starvation.

The weight on Evan's shoulders grew.

Bill caught him in the entryway. "Hold on, Sam."

Sam stopped, his hand on the door. It, too, was cold. Not as cold as the stone that surrounded it or the icy air outside.

Small swirls of it blew back in from under and around the door. It set his teeth to chattering. How he longed for a thick winter coat then, like a bear or a sheep hide wrapped around him.

"Bill. I've been meaning to talk to you." Sam looked for an escape, but couldn't see one. No one that was easy, at least. He was going to try one anyway. "I was just going to the workshop to see how things were going."

"I'll come with you, then. Nothing like seeing a boat being built, eh?" Bill slapped him on the back. "Lead the way."

"Certainly." Sam hunkered down and pushed open the door. The wind howled in, nearly covering him with a big puff of snow that stung his eyes and got in his mouth.

It was bitter cold outside, and Sam pushed forward through the deep drift at the door.

How to ask it? He needed Bill's help. Or, rather, he needed the masons to help build what he envisioned, and they wouldn't do anything without Bill saying so first. Either way, the man following him through feet deep snow was important to him and the potential survival of the castle.

They pushed into the workshop, and Sam took deep breaths of the slightly warmer air. How he wished there was a fire crackling in the hearth again, casting a merry warmth to steal away this cold.

The frame of the boat was nearly finished now, and Trent was on top fitting a lap joint. It wasn't the best looking boat Sam had ever seen, but it was going to work.

He hoped.

"That's it?" Bill asked.

"Now give us some respect," Ned said, turning to them. "Unless you want to find yourself helping."

"We've run into a few...complications," Sam said. There was no use hiding the fact now, Bill could plainly see that there wasn't enough wood to finish the hull. "And as much as I'd like to move the crane over to the wall, we might need it for something else."

"And that would be?" Bill asked.

"The southwest tower. We need to scavenge the beams in it," Trent said.

Sam sighed. he was hoping to have phrased it a little better. "He's right. I've gone over it many times. We just don't have what we need."

"But the Keep does," Bill said. Sam nodded. "Since we've started down this path, I don't see any other way. We can help."

Bill walked around the boat as Sam worked his fingers to keep the cold out of the joints. He was hungry, like everyone else.

"Shall we go up there to see?"

Sam would have preferred not to. Not in this wind.

They stood at the top of the unfinished tower. As he suspected, the wind was brutally cold up here and blew right through him. Sam couldn't stop shivering and held himself tight.

Bill had a thicker coat on. Like everything else related to Bill, Sam had no idea where he got it from.

"A few courses would do it. Shame to see all the hard work undone."

"If there was another way…" Sam wished it had never come to this, that they were able to build in peace.

"No chance of sneaking out late at night, harvesting a few trees, and bringing them back in?" Bill asked.

"Let's get out of this wind," Sam said, retreating back down the unfinished stairs. He sighed as he got beneath the protection of the walls. Snow drifted down the stairs. Up here the warm air escaped up the opening from the castle below. Bill followed, not as affected by the cold stone beneath his feet. His shoes looked thick and not as worn as everyone else.

"It is a cold winter," Bill said, tightening up his collar. "Shame about Nathula."

"You knew him well?"

"Well enough. The Overseer is going Sam." They were withing the protection of the tower now, the cold and snow of outside blunted.

Sam turned to face Bill. "I was afraid you were behind that." Bill shrugged. "Why?"

"He wanted to go. He gives us the best chance of salvation, should he survive."

"And the Duke loses a key ally."

"I wouldn't put it that way. Now that you mention it, though..." Bill looked up at the ceiling.

"You can't do it," Sam said.

"I'll do what I need to stay alive." Bill's face hardened, his eyes snapping to Sam's. "Do you have the resolve to do the same?"

"What good would I be if my life is all I considered? I've been that man before."

"So you want to be known as the savior, then—the man who sacrificed himself? Such a self-righteous man," Bill mocked.

Sam's face felt too tight, like a hide stretched on the tanning rack. "I can see coming to ask you to help wasn't the right decision."

The nook they had taken refuge in was dark and tucked int eh corner of the tower, the door to the rest of the Keep just on the wall behind them.

No one came up here, no one ventured this far. In his rage Sam thought about killing Bill, and leaving his body in the corner.

The flashing thought frightened him at how easy the thought came. he took a deep breath, trying to control the rage and anger and helplessness that fought inside him.

Bill had taken a step back, and was crouched into a ready stance, a few movements away from a fighting position.

It was silly. *How am I a threat to Bill.* Then Sam looked down. His fists were balled up, and he looked like he was about to attack.

"I mean no offense," Sam said, relaxing himself. He was reminded of the fact that Bill was afraid of him, something he wasn't sure was true up until that very moment.

"None take," Bill said, relaxing into a more natural and carefree posture. But Sam could tell there was something about him that was ready, coiled like a snake ready to spring.

This wasn't going to get him where he needed to go with Bill, and certainly wouldn't get him goodwill. The thought of him asking about the plans for revolt was too much for Sam to think of.

"Instead of fighting, I'd propose we work together. I have some plans for expanding the denseness of the castle that we can work on even now."

"I heard of your plans," Bill said. "I wasn't impressed by them."

Sam smiled. "You don't have to be. They just have to work."

20

TEMPTATIONS

"What you're asking for is too much. No way am I going to ask my masons to go out into the cold and build a bunch of walls we aren't going to use."

Thy had moved to a cellar room in the castle, previously filled with food. It had a few stacks of grain left, and not much else, but it was warm and out of the way.

Bill, however, had failed to move.

"I'm telling you it's going to work. The gate is the weak point, and always has been. The Belmarch aren't stupid, they know that too." Sam sat on a makeshift stool, a small barrel.

Bill sat opposed, on an overturned crate. "They haven't tried the gate before, other than the ram."

"That doesn't mean they aren't going to try it again." Sam rubbed his head. He was starting to get a dull throb behind his eyes. It wasn't pleasant, combined with his hunger.

"They've gone for the walls every other time though, why would they suddenly get through our gate, and how would they do it?"

"How many sieges have you gone through?" Sam snapped. Bill's eyes narrowed. Sam took a deep breath and smoothed out his voice. "The gate is a few inches of wood. The walls are a few feet of rock. Which one is going to be easier to get through?"

"Up and over both of them."

"It hasn't worked yet. They know we can repulse them."

"Not if we're all half-dead and starved."

He had a point, but one Sam wasn't going to cede. "For all we know they don't have the supplies to keep this siege up. They might try to get through the next time the weather is good enough to allow them to attack," Sam said.

Bill snorted. "They'd be fools to attack before spring."

"Unless they took us by surprise."

"In that case your walls won't help us."

"It's a trap, Bill. Even you can see that."

"And what if this trap springs, and doesn't work. What then? We've invited them within the walls and we're all dead."

It was frustrating trying to reason with him. They had been going at it back and forth for what seemed like hours. Each point was argued over, each time Sam tried to show him the error of his thinking.

It just felt like he was going around in circles, but he couldn't appeal to the Overseer. Bill had too much sway over him, and the Overseer had made it clear this was between them.

Nor could he talk to the Duke and try and convince him either. Sam was afraid doing so would set off the spark that lit the wildfire of revolt.

So, here he was, sitting in a damp cellar in the dark, breathing in moldy air that tasted rotten. He even though he heard the squeak of rats, and saw things out of the corner of his eye, but could never see it when he went to look.

Was he destined to go around these same points with Bill forever?

"This isn't working," Sam said, crossing his arms. Up until now he had tried to keep his posture relaxed and open. "What do you propose instead? Should we let them take us without doing anything?"

"No. We fight them."

"And when we can't fight them anymore, when we can't hold them aback any longer, what do we do then?"

Bill paused. "We fall back to the Keep and keep fighting them."

"With no source of water?" The well was in the courtyard, well outside the walls of the Keep.

"Then we have to have help. Someone is going to have to sweep the Belmarch away from us, and keep us alive."

Sam wondered about that, if it was even possible. The King had to have known that something was wrong by now. "They know we're in trouble," Sam said, in barely a whisper. "You and I both know that."

Bill considered him, looking at him with that studying look that told Sam there was something deeper going on behind them. Bill knew.

"I've thought about it on watch. In the cold, when I couldn't feel my fingers." Sam saw Bill flex his own hand at his words. "Why would they leave us, why would they abandon us here?"

"They haven't abandoned us," Bill said, but his voice wasn't confident.

"The Belmarch aren't the most pressing matter in Chathem. You know the rumors as well as I."

"The eastern raiders have never been a threat to Chathem," Bill said.

"And yet, here we are with no supplies and no reinforcements." Sam felt a chill run up his spine at his own words, words he had kept deep inside, never wishing to speak them.

But here they were, pouring out of him like water.

"We are well and truly alone. I can't count on anyone going for help to be successful."

Bill sat, his shoulders slumped. Sam knew in that moment that Bill was counting on rescue. He believed in the power of the king, but didn't know the reality of their situation.

Chathem didn't have a strong monarchy. It was barely a collection of states held together, and the current King wasn't strong enough to do anything but keep them together.

No, Sam suspected the Duke of Hornblood was the real driver of the castle construction, and its primary benefactor. At the extreme northern end of Chathem, the Dukedom of the Hornbloods bore the brunt of the Belmarch invasions for generations.

But, it appeared they had given all they could, and their support was dried up. Or, he suspected, they had lost their favor at court, and their source of treasure to keep the construction going.

"Think about it. The lack of resources, less and less workers coming in when we needed more and more," Sam said. The musty, rotten smell was overpowering, and it was making his headache worse. "No one is coming to save us Bill. Were' going to have to do this on our own."

Bill hesitated, then spoke. "You don't know that for sure. Bedsides, even if you were right then we wouldn't stand a chance at all."

"We could buy time."

"There would be no hope for us."

"I've thought about that," Sam said. "I've seen wild things happen, things I never expected. Things that turned the tide of battle from certain defeat to victory." The red eagle taken down by a single arrow. "We could plan for the worst and give us the best chance we would have."

"You might be right, but I don't think so."

Sam stood up and stretched his legs. He was getting tired and needed to sleep before his watch. As warm as it was down here, he was considering bringing his rotten and flea ridden blanket down here to do it. "I don't have time to try and convince you. Maybe when we've sent the Overseer on his journey downriver you will see the benefit to my plan."

"Your plan will take too long to build."

Sam shrugged. "You're making excuses, not good arguments. Why don't we call it a night and think it over." Sam walked to the door and opened it, but paused as he walked out.

Bill was still sitting in the dark, the single candle he had produced burning in the corner. It struggled to stay alive, the flame dancing on the edge of the wick. Its rays went less than halfway across the room before dying out.

"I'll ask again, have you ever survived a siege before?" Sam asked.

Bill turned his head but said nothing.

"Good night, Bill."

Evan tore through the stack of books in the next few days, his workouts getting longer and his muscles adapting to them.

It felt good to get his movements back, to feel real improvement once more. The first form was more fluid, and easier to perform than it had been, and the others were improving with every practice session.

The days turned into a blur, not knowing when the sun came up and the sun went down, he read when he could see and he lit the candle when he couldn't. The sky was so overcast so often he wasn't sure if it was night sometimes, or just a lack of sun.

He longed to see it again, and feel it's burning rays upon his face. The feeling was even more intense than other winters, and it was because he was stuck indoors.

His only interruptions were mealtimes and visits from the Overseer. Evan hated those the most.

It only cemented the feeling he had that he had no control of the situation. The only joy he took in it was the look on Rhys face the first time he had come in to see him reading.

"Surprised?" Evan had asked him. The man's eyebrows had almost reached his receding hairline before he had gotten control of them.

"Pleasantly," Rhys had said.

Even now the memory helped to dull the feeling of hopelessness, and the draw of the wine.

That had been the hardest thing to handle. Every morning Evan woke up and thought about asking Barger or Rhys to take it away, but every night he came to the end of the day not able to say it.

He sat in his chair one night looking at it. Four bottles, neatly arranged. Untouched since Barger had drunk one glass.

The candlelight flickered in the reflection on the glass. How much money was poured into those vessels alone? More than any one of the workers in the castle would see in their lifetimes.

He could just make out the faint line of the wine inside. Dark, almost as black as the night sky in the green glass. He looked away, his eyes hurting from staring so hard.

Evan put a hand on his head. How many nights had he wasted in that smooth liquid? How many years had he abused it?

No, I never abused it. It was just a drink, a taste to ease the pain.

The pain of failure, the pain of being alone. Even now he wished for Yand, the closest thing to a friend he had ever had. He was a hard mentor, but fair in what mattered.

They never shared a friend's discussion, but there was a familiarly that Evan longed for now.

It would all be so easy. Just a few sips. It had been so long since he had taken a drink. He swallowed the saliva that had built up in his mouth.

The warm, sweet notes of the grape, the bitter aftertaste as it went down. That lingering sensation that took on so many different kinds of flavors. Oak, butter, nuts.

The wine he had brought with him had been some of the best Hornblood had to offer, the local vintage made from the hardy grapes that grew in the glades of the forest. Starved of light from the canopy of the trees, the grapes were small and puny looking, but packed with flavor that only made it better when it was fermented.

Evan licked his lips, imagining the wine washing over them and into his waiting mouth. He put a finger to them, rubbed therm.

They were cracked and dry. *A hint of wine would do them good.*

He snatched his finger away. *No, I can't.* The room felt hot, and his head spun with the longing. Why *did* it have to be this hard?

Why I do I resist it? It isn't wrong. Another voice spoke up inside him, warning him of what had happened so many times before.

The ditches he had woken up in, the pigsties he found himself covered in. Mud and filth piled up on his body, his head and body rebelling against sunlight and noise.

The shame he felt the next day after what he heard from his drinking companions, and the sidelong glances they sent him with smirks lingering on their lips, just out of reach. The whispers behind his back.

Evan bit his lip, then turned his chair around, out of sight from the cabinet and the looming bottles. It wasn't the first time this had happened, he struggled through this every night only to be haunted in his dreams by it.

It's just a liquid. Even now, looking away, he could see it. He saw it tumbling out of the bottle, filling up the goblet, shining in the candlelight.

He felt himself being pulled from his chair, as if his body had a mind of its own, but he knew it was his own action that was doing it.

Evan had such a horrible feeling overpower him. He couldn't stop it.

With shaking hands, he took a bottle and a goblet, and poured a glass of wine.

21

MIST OF TIME

Evan closed his eyes when the wine his lips. Even before then the smell of the wine was overpowering and heady.

The taste, however, wasn't what he imagined it would be. It wasn't as sweet as he remembered, or as filling. The mouthful went down his throat and all the way to his stomach, settling there as a cold lump for a second or two.

He had expected something to happen, something bad. When it never materialized, he took another drink, then turned back to go to his seat.

Evan froze mid-step. For a second, he thought his father was on his chair, sitting and watching him sternly, but he was mistaken.

No one was there.

But above his seat the crest of the Hornbloods looked down on him. The Tree of Everling spread out its branches, shaking them as if they were fists at him.

He was transported across time and space to his first Midnight Watch. The candles flickered in their lanterns, the long train processing through the woods.

They were bare and desolate. He remembered being carried of their branches, that they might reach out and pluck him from his mother's grip.

Evan moved closer, clasping his mother's hand even tighter.

"Still, Evan," she said, in a soothing voice, with a hint of sternness. He peered up at here, seeing her head illuminated against the backdrop of the thick, black night sky. "It will be over soon."

The Tree still had its leaves, even now in the dead of winter with a frosting of snow. It crunched as they gathered around the base of it, the headstones scattered among the gnarly old roots.

It smelled of winter, and felt it. The icy wind stung his little eyes and burrowed behind his coat and down his neck. Someone was saying something, but he couldn't hear very well.

He caught parts of the speech, from his grandfather perched at the tallest root of the tree. The rest of the family was scattered out around the tree, the women and children on one side and his father and the men on the other.

He had been promised that one day he would join his father's side, both in life and in death.

As his grandfather spoke the first leaf of the tree came down, shaken free finally by the winter winds.

It fell in front of Evan, as black as night. Before his mother could stop him, he stooped down and touched it.

"No!"

It was too late. Evan had the rough stem in his hand, the leaf almost as big as his head held up before him.

"Cursed," his aunt Delores hissed. "You have seen it all, he is cursed!"

"Put it down, Evan," his father said in his stern, cold voice. Evan dropped it, and the leaf fell once more into the snow.

Tears stung at his eyes, and he could stop the hot liquid from coming. His whole family was talking now, breaking the ritual silence that had pervaded before.

"We continue with the ritual, everyone return to their places," his grandfather had said. The voices died down and everyone returned to their original spots, but Evan clutched at his mother's leg.

She didn't say anything to comfort him, only held his head. Grandfather waited until the tree had shed all its' leaves and then picked up the biggest one and offered it into the fire burning in the stone pit near the trunk.

"We offer our thanks and praise. We ask you, the ancestors of the wood, to bring us peace and prosper us. Bring our enemies to their knees and our friends to our table." Grandfather held his hands up as the smoke drifted up through the wood, swirling around them with the aroma Evan couldn't describe, but would never forget.

And then he was back in his study. Evan was shaking, the goblet clutched in one hand. He was on his knees. How he got there, he wasn't sure.

"Cursed." He remembered the words, floated back through his mind from his childhood. He had done that which was reserved for his grandfather, the patriarch of the family.

He had brought dishonor upon his line, and cursed it forever.

He was the reason they were under attack. Had it not been for his coming the castle would have been built in time and fully manned, ready to propel the attackers and send the Belmarch back into their land where they belonged.

A low moan escaped his lips. Evan squeezed his eyes shut and brought the goblet back to his lips.

His trembling hand splashed wine up onto his face, little drips of it that ran down his nose and eyes.

"Cursed," he said again, after he had taken a deep draw. More and more he wanted to drink the whole cup, and then the rest of the bottle, but something inside him held him back.

Was it the look in his fathers' eye? The feel of his mother's touch? Something had changed that day.

But why had his father and mother not cast him off at that moment? he deserved to be cut off from the family, to be thrown to the wolves and be devoured. That was the punishment for his crime, and it had been enacted before.

Evan held the goblet to his lips and drained it. Wine spilled on his shirt, but he didn't care. The smell of it pervaded his senses, pushed away that memory of the Everling smoke out of his mind.

He had gone back, year after year, and never touched a leaf again, but the damage had already been done. It was finished.

He was cursed.

He was destined to ruin. A prophecy and a warning come to fruition in the cold, damp room he now occupied.

What could he do? The goblet was empty now, and he let it slip from his fingers with a clatter. It rolled away from him, and Evan fell to the floor.

He imagined a life that would have been had he not done it. He would have the love of his mother still, and the succession secure. There would have been friends, waiting for him after a long campaign, or joining him in it.

And that was all gone now, never to be. He would drink his cup of suffering, and drink it to the fullest, to die in this place a lonely, broken man.

"Your Highness," Barger said, a note of panic in his voice. Hands were on his back, pulling him to his side.

"Leave me be," Evan groaned. Barger's wide-open eyes were filled with concern. "I'm not worth helping."

His eyes flashed to the cup and the wind spilled upon Evan's clothes. "I'll help you to your bed."

The wine had gone to his head now, bringing in a buzz that made his muscles loose and hampered his inhibitions.

Barger shouldn't bee here, shouldn't see him like this. Evan struggled to his feet, and pushed him away.

"Go. I don't want you here." Evan looked around wildly. Was his father here?

"You aren't in a good state," Barger said. Evan saw a bottle near the goblet, a tiny drop at the mouth.

It was empty. *How much have I had to drink?* Evan didn't remember having that much. Somewhere in the last hour though, he recalled pouring more than one glass. *Was that after the memory?*

From the swimming in his head, he thought it might. The room was wobbling, and the walked to the closest chair at the table pushed up against the wall.

Barger was there at his elbow, guiding him to sit. He collapsed into the chair, the hard back pushing into his spine.

"What do you say?" Evan asked, as Barger went to clean up the mess. The servant was on his hands and knees, scrubbing with a rag he had produced from somewhere.

"Pardon, Your Highness?"

Evan waved a hand toward the door. " I know what they think. That I can't do anything right, that I'm useless. That they're better off without me. What do you think?"

Barger considered his words carefully. "It wouldn't be right-"

"Blast it all, answer the question!"

"If Your Highness insists." Barger bowed, infuriating Evan even more. The haze of drunkenness drifted through his vision, but his anger and hatred kept the worst of it at bay.

"I don't think you are useless. These last few days something has changed in you. In all my years I have never seen you read, or train as hard as you have, or even talk to me like you have these last few days." Barger didn't look pleased and kept his eyes on the ground.

Evan didn't know what to think. Barger had spoken what he thought, but Evan had asked for it. Had he really gone all these years without speaking to him?

he knew it was true, even if he didn't want to believe it. Evan licked his lips. "I'm cursed, you know. That's why this has happened." He gestured around him with his arms. "You have me to blame for all your troubles." Had he not taken that leaf, had he just left it on the ground like he was supposed to...

What would his life look like then?

"I've known the bottom of a cup. There isn't any good in it," Barger said. He was still cleaning, hands on the floor, eyes downcast. The wine had fully taken Evan's mind now. He thought he heard a note of sorrow in that voice, but it couldn't be true. Barger had always intoned his words in a cool, calm way with no emotions. "You don't want to go down that path."

Evan stared at him. He was hardly older than Evan was, or so he first thought. But there were creases as the corner of the man's eyes, something he hadn't seen before.

Why was he talking to the servant? Why was he speaking this way?

"I'd like to be left alone," Evan said. "Finish that and get out." he would have another taste, another sip. It would help ease his suffering, help him to feel better.

"As you wish, your highness." Something flashed across Barger's face, and was gone a moment later. Evan blinked, but Barger was still there, still as calm as always.

The man finished his cleaning, then stood. He walked to the door.

As he did Evan watched him go. His eyes traveled momentarily to the floor, and the book caught his attention.

The *History* had fallen somehow, either knocked down by Evan or Barger as he helped him. It was open to the chapter on Miral, the illustration of the former King staring at him.

Behind him, a tree that looked like the Tree of Everling spread out its branches, blood red leaves upon them. It seemed to be embracing the man.

From a failure, all the way to one of the greatest Kings. Evan put his hand over his eyes, trying to blot out the eyes that stared at him.

Mocking him.

Telling him he was a failure. That he would never amount to anything. That his father was right.

That his family curse was real. He was the last and only Hornblood to reside in this castle. The only Hornblood to keep watch, and fail in the act of it.

All hope drained from him then, like wine in the cup he had drawn from.

Emotion racked his body, and Evan couldn't help but let out a sob. He had tried so hard and had come up short.

Above him, his family crest mocked him. He turned to it, tried to tear it from the wall, but he was too drunk.

Evan couldn't get his hands around it, and slipped to the floor.

His head hit the book, dazing him. Evan pulled himself up from the ground.

The page had turned. It was the moment Miral had snuck from the camp, the pivotal moment when he was at his weakest.

The artist had drawn fear in his eyes, a cloak pulled up to hide his identity. But there was something else too, a sunrise.

It spilled out in red and yellow. Evan remembered how the story ended, how he had come back from nothing, an outcast, the hunted, and had prevailed.

Barger hadn't left. He was standing over him, a look of worry on his face.

Maybe there is hope for me, after all. There would be a tomorrow. As long as he didn't give up hope, there would be another day.

"Barger," Evan said, holding his throbbing head. "Take the wine."

22

A BOAT

"It is done."

Sam knelt by the boat, unseaworthy by his estimation. "And she'll hold?" he asked. "I'd bet my life on it," Kerien said.

Ned gave him a look. "She'll be fine, for as long as we need her to be. We didn't have everything we needed..." They had stuffed her joints with sawdust and wood shavings. Ned had wanted to use rope and fiber mixed with tar, but they had little rope to spare and no tar to speak of, so they made do instead.

"But you've done a fine job with her." Sam tried to look through the gaps, see daylight behind them, but couldn't. "It just looks...""You don't mean it looks ugly..." Kerien said, his face darkening." Shorter than I expected," Sam said, trying to smooth over any insult he might have unintentionally given.

The workshop was cold, like everything else, and now almost empty. Stacks of wood should have been piled up on one side, but there were only a few sticks. Everything had gone into this boat, including the beam they had removed from the Keep that now functioned as the main brace.

The rest had been consumed in fire two nights ago, the coldest yet. Sam was glad for it too, because had they not more than one wouldn't have survived the night.

169

He shivered thinking of it now. The workshop didn't smell the same as it used to. He didn't know if it was the cold that made it different or the lack of wood and dust, but he didn't like it.

"We could launch it tonight?" Sam asked, looking up from his inspection. Trent was with them too, everyone but Archie. The thought of him made him think of Belinda. *Poor child.*

"If we had to, yes." Ned put up a gnarled hand to her prow. "She took everything I knew, and then some, to get her together. Make sure you take care of her.

"We'll do it soon. The sooner the better." Sam frowned. He would have to get Bill and his masons to finish their work. "We'll take down the crane and see how far we can get."

Bill had wanted to do his work a long time ago, but Sam had insisted he not do it. There was too much risk in it.

The Belmarch might see them working on it and get interested, find out a way to watch the river and even get close enough to foil their plan. Sam wasn't sure how they could get away with it, but didn't want to take the risk. In the end Bill had agreed, but only after much arguing and bickering.

The man was like a stone wall himself. Hard to get through unless you could break him down.

So, instead of taking out the merlons, he only prepared for it, having a mason take out some of the wall stones where the crane would sit and remove some of the backing rocks. The rest of it would have to be taking out in the same night as everything else.

The only thing they had that winter was helping on was how long night was lasting. The days were already growing longer now, but the long nights were still here.

he wasn't looking forward to the night, but the moon was going to be full soon. It might help with light, at the very least.

"Let's get her out of here and up the hill," Sam said. "Should be easy enough to carry."

Ned and Kerien looked at each other.

"What?" Sam asked.

"I'm not so sure about that..." Kerien said.

"We used a lot of wood. Dense wood," Ned added.

"We have four. Let's try and see. Trent, get on that side, you two on this one." They repositioned, each man taking a corner. It was hard to grip the round bottom, and Sam struggled to find something to hold onto.

Finally, he used his opened hand to get some grip, the other positioned over the lip of the boat.

"Everyone ready?" hearing affirmative replies Sam gave the order.

He pulled the boat, but it didn't move. Sam strained harder, but still nothing.

"Is everyone pulling?"

"Yes. It's heavier than it looks," Ned said. The others grunted too.

"Let me reposition." Sam changed his stance, trying to wrap his arms around the front of it. They had put it on blocks during the building, which gave him enough room to crouch down.

With better grip they tried again, but failed. For a while they tried to lift it up, to no avail.

"All we're doing is wearing ourselves out," Trent said, after what seemed like the tenth try.

He was right, and Sam knew it. They couldn't keep wasting their strength like this, especially with how hungry they were.

Sam's stomach always felt empty now, the rations getting tighter and tighter. He stepped back to get a better look.

It was in the middle of the workshop, the workbenches pushed to the sides to accommodate it. It was about twice as long as he was tall, and a quarter that side to side.

They should be able to lift it. It wasn't that big.

When he cast his gaze over the others though, he had an inkling of why.

None of them had an ounce of fat on their bodies. They were gaunt faced, cheeks thin, with sunken eyes.

It wasn't that the boat that was the problem. It was the reasons why they had stopped training days ago, why there were fewer sentries on the walls than they really should have.

They were starving to death.

Sam closed his eyes, trying to blot out the image. *When had this happened?*

he knew it was going to be this way, had feared it ever since they had been trapped inside these walls.

Deep down he had known all along, but it was this thing that had made it real to him.

"I-" Sam found himself at a loss for words.

"We'll get more help," Trent said. "With enough of us we can move it."

Why hadn't he thought of that? He recovered from the momentary shock and sadness that washed over him, and then nodded.

"That's a good idea, Trent." About double their number should do the trick, if they all hadn't lost as much strength as the carpenters.

He had to feel something, ground himself back in the real world. Sam reached out and held the prow of the boat. *This was the beam we took from the Keep.*

The wood was cold, but solid. His hand was perpetually frozen. Some men had lost feeling in theirs, and their feet and toes, but the rough wood was there under his fingertips, reminding him of the world.

A cold gust of wind blew through the workshop, cutting through him. If they had a fire going, it would have put it out. Fire—and a good side of mutton. Sam would have done anything for it at that moment.

"Who are we going to ask?" Ned asked.

"Bill will let us use the masons. They've lost..." He coughed and tried again. "They're the strongest out of all of us, except the smiths."

But they too had lost their strength too. Perhaps not all, but enough.

"What about the guardsmen? I don't feel right asking Bill," Ned said.

"I don't either, but I'm not sure they'd help us."

"Let me talk to them first," Trent said. Sam turned to him, surprised. "I have a favor that I can use."

"A favor?" Sam asked, knitting his eyebrows together. *Since when has Trent done anything to get a favor in return?*

"Yes. I'd rather not talk about why."

"Then you ask," Sam said.

"Are we just going to wait here?" Kerien asked after Trent had left.

"Got anything better to do?" Ned asked. He had sat down on his stool, tucked away in the corner and out of the stray gusts that ran through the workshop.

"We could wait inside," Kerien said, rubbing his arms. Today wasn't as cold as it had been the past few days, but snow still covered the ground a few inches thick.

"Give him a few minutes. If he isn't back soon, we'll head back to the Keep. I'm sure he'll find us." Sam turned to Ned. "Do you know anything about this favor?"

"First I've heard about it."

"It's strange."

"I don't think so," Kerien said, also sitting down beside Ned to share some body heat. "He's been standing extra watches at night. Says he has to figure something out."

"Extra watches?" That would explain why Sam hadn't seen him in the workshop as much. Come to think of it, he was on the southern wall a lot more than normal. Why that hadn't stood out to him, he wasn't sure.

"Mostly the guardsman near the gatehouse," Kerien said, rubbing his hands together.

Sam joined them. Together they pressed their backs up against each other. It felt good to be a little warm again in one part of his body.

He had forgotten what that felt like.

"What is he looking for?" Sam asked.

Kerien shrugged. "He hasn't told me, but it is something to do with the Belmarch camp. He's always staring off at it. That, and the forest."

Sam wondered as they drifted into silence. A few moments later crunches on snow drifted into the workshop, the sound of more than a few pairs of feet.

Trent ducked in, followed by Mathew and a few other guardsmen. Others also trailed in, six more in all.

"This is it?" Mathew asked. "Shouldn't be too hard to move if we all work together."

They all took positions around the boat, ten pairs of hands beneath it. After everyone was ready Sam gave the signal.

After a brief moment of doubt, the boat lifted up off its resting blocks. Sam instructed them where to go, and they pushed out into the sunny courtyard through the workshop flaps.

The warm sun felt good on his face, and Sam almost stopped to soak it in, but was quickly brought back to humility by the sharp gusts of wind that stole that warmth away.

They pushed through the snow and up the hill, stopping twice to set it down and catch their breath. There was less than a hundred feet from the workshop to the place where they would build the crane.

The snow slowed them down. It had drifted up against the wall a few feet high, pushed there by the constant wind that even now knocked snow into his face.

Sam squinted against the swirls and pushed on. They made it and dropped the boat down.

"Thank you," Sam said, turning back to the new arrivals. Everyone was breathing hard but wore smiles on their faces.

"We owe Trent," Mathew said, clapping the young man on the back. "He deserves more than we could give him." The others agreed, but the wind was too bad, and drove them out of the sun and back into the protective walls of the Keep.

Sam hung back as the group walked through the yard. He was still surprised and marveled at Trent, surrounded by the others.

Ned joined him, walking slowly. The wind had died down somewhat, but the sun had been covered by a thin layer of clouds.

"Something's changed in him, Ned."

"Are you sure it's in him?" Drifts of snow brushed across the ground.

"No. Not anymore. I don't want him to have to grow up, to be a man that faces this hardship and suffering."

Ned didn't say anything. He just walked alongside him. The others slipped into the Keep.

"I don't know if this will work. I don't know if we'll survive."

"Can't say anything different," Ned said, looking up into the sky. "This is my last winter, Sam. I can feel it in my bones."

"No. You can't say that."

"I'm old, Sam. I've lived my life. I've had my time." Ned nodded toward the others. "This is his time."

Sam felt hollow.

"Don't mourn for me when I'm gone."

Sam's voice caught in his throat. "I'm not sure we won't be going together."

Ned turned to him, a fierce fire in his eyes. "You'll survive, and you'll protect all the others. Promise me that—humor an old man."

Sam couldn't. He couldn't say the words.

23

LEAVING

When Barger walked out Evan felt a weight lift off his shoulders. The bottles went with him, to be dispensed and poured out if need be. Evan wasn't sure what was going to happen to them, and some part of him cared.

Some part of him mourned for it, but the greater portion of him was different. He had changed. Nothing had changed him for him, as many times he had wished for something to make him different.

It was the same way with Yand, when his father had ordered him to serve as a bodyguard and trainer. Evan had hoped that Yand would make him better, change him from who he was.

Evan pondered this in his study as the sun went down and the light failed. A knock on his door roused him.

Head still affected from the wine, Evan bade whoever it was to enter and rose to his feet. He closed the *History of Chathem* softly, with reverent affection for the pages.

He was surprised to see Rhys enter. "Good evening, Your Highness," Rhys said.

"I wasn't expecting you," Evan said. They had already had their meeting earlier in the day. "I don't assume anything has changed in the inventory?"

"I'm not here for our normal discussion." Evan bade him come and sit at the table, still pushed out of the way from his training session, but with room enough from them both to take a seat.

Rhys had dark circles under his eyes and moved like a man with little rest. "I have something to tell you," he said after they were seated across from one another. "I'm going soon, tonight if we can manage it."

"Going?" Evan furrowed his brow. "Going where?"

"Away. Down the river."

"On the river? However will you get there?" Evan imagined the once large figure sneaking out of the gate in the middle of the night. "And what boat will you take?"

"The carpenters have been working on a boat for the last few weeks," Rhys said, hands folded in his lap. "It's in the courtyard now, next to the wall. We're going to lift it up and over the wall to the river."

A boat? Here in the castle? Evan couldn't believe his ears, and stared at Rhys without blinking. "What is going on?"

"I should have told you earlier," Rhys said. "I apologize. We've been putting this plan in place for a while, and I wasn't sure until tonight if they would be able to do it." Rhys shook his head, a small smile playing at the corner of his lips. "They seem to hate each other, but suit each other so well."

Rhys filled him in. At the end of it Evan sat, somewhat in shock.

"And so, you intent to be the one to go."

"That's right. Who else would we send?" Rhys sighed, face changing into the old man he was for a second. He regained his composure quickly.

Thoughts were racing through Evan. Feelings and emotions mixed in. Leave the castle, and actually survive. It could be him.

Would it be the best thing for everyone? No one else would have the authority he had, even Overseer Rhys.

"Why you?" Evan's mouth was dry, and his hands shook.

"You are needed here." Evan knew what the answer was going to be, but didn't want to hear it. He looked away.

"No one needs me," he said bitterly. "You said it yourself. I'm one step away from being killed."

"Perhaps that has changed."

"I don't see how it could have."

"Your actions, and inactions, spread faster through the castle. Faster than you think," Rhys said.

Evan had a lump in his throat. "I know I've been a poor Duke, and an even worse leader. I should have done things differently." Evan looked into Rhys' eyes. "What can I do to make things better without you here to help me?"

Rhys considered his words, meeting his gaze. Evan was afraid he wouldn't say anything at all, but he did finally speak. "When you came here, I wasn't sure what to think of you. A spoiled young man, unsure of his place in the world, without a care for those beneath him. Is that the same man that sits here before me?"

"Yes, I'm afraid it is."

Rhys smiled. "Which tells me you have changed. I know you think you need me here, but I am better used on the task that is set before me. When I get to the capitol I will find a way to bring help, don't doubt that for a second."

The gloom of the night, banished by a candle Rhys had lit when he came in, pervaded the conversation and the atmosphere. Evan had a hard time looking pas it, and the quiet of the night. The stillness seemed to flow from the stones themselves.

He was probably right. Evan wasn't much use to the court to begin with, and was an embarrassment to his father when he was there. He had few acquaintances, and even fewer friends there. Even throwing his family name around might not help, even with the threat of a Belmarch invasion.

Rhys was the right choice, and he knew it. A lower-level messenger wouldn't have the pull to get them help right away, and they needed it to survive the winter.

"Tell me what I have to do, before you leave. Teach me what I need to know." Evan stared into Rhys' eyes, trying to take his knowledge and wisdom into himself.

"There is little for me to teach you that Yand hasn't already taught. What I can tell you is that it might be time to take your place among your people again, as a humble and rightful ruler."

Like Miral of old, disgraced and weak, rising up to become the best of what the Hornbloods had to offer. Evan saw a glimmer of hope in that future, one that could happen for him.

"I'm not sure I can accomplish it, but I will try."

24

PREPARATION UNFOLDS

Sam stood on the battlements in the late afternoon sun. The wind had died down, giving a blessedly peaceful quality to the day. The warmth of the sun infused his body with life, dispelling the cold from the side of his body the sun faced.

The air was crisp and clean, tasting cold and sweet after the dank air of the Keep. He took a long look around at the barren trees. They blocked the view, so many sticks piled up on each other, but gave hints of what lay beyond.

The mason's hammers rang out. They were working on the merlons as quietly as they could, removing the bottom layer of mortar from the stone. When night came, they would remove the rocks one by one with cloth wrapped hands, but for now they only prepared.

Ned had recommended only a few men up on the tower to disassemble the crane, and Sam was glad they had followed his sage advice. Even now, with the three other carpenters working on it, Sam winced, hoping they didn't alert the Belmarch to the plan.

The sun was already almost at the horizon, given a few more minutes it would be. Bill stood beside him, supervising the work.

"Do you think they will notice?" Bill asked.

Sam looked over to the white smoke that rose into the air above their camp. They had plenty of fuel for cooking and warmth, surrounded by the timber forests that were theirs by right.

Sam hated to think of it, but remembered watching them fell large oaks and drag them back to their camp. They chopped it up, not for building, but for another purpose.

To burn.

Destroy, maim, kill. That was what the Belmarch were here for, and they were good at it. Even the forests and the land couldn't stand up to them.

He mourned for the loss of the trees. They would have made good beams and timbers. Solid after generations of growing, he would have shaped them to fit into the careful constructed holes in the stone wall so that it could continue, building towers that reached up to touch the sky.

But that was all gone, for now.

One day, it may happen again. It was a glimmer of hope, and one he held onto with a fierce passion and desire.

"We must do it whether they notice or not," Sam said at last, after he had broken free of those painful memories. He still feared they would never survive.

This was not a sound plan, but the only one he could think of with any real shot of success. Like an archer in the woods, starving and depending only on their skill to survive, they had one shot to take at this.

"A lot of hope rides on this one act then," Bill said. Sam nodded, grimacing.

The three figures on the half-finished watchtower slipped down, beneath the sight lines of the enemies. *They must be done.*

Like the masons, the carpenters were waiting until the night had fallen in earnest to enact their plan. They needed the cover of darkness and surprise to give them as much of as advantage as they could.

And as much of a head start for the Overseer to get as far away downriver as they could.

There was no going back now. They would have one shot at this, he feared, before the food would run out and the starvation would take them.

"The river isn't calm," Bill said. He was right. It was swollen, and turbulent. Not the most that Sam had seen this winter, but not nearly as peaceful as eh would have liked it to be.

"The Overseer is a boatman. Or so you said."

"So I did, and so I believe."

"Do you still really intend to carry through with it?" Sam asked, turning as the masons went back inside, as much done with the wall as they could until the appointed hour.

"Do you see any other option to make it out of here alive?"

"Yes, we get reinforcements and rescue from the very man you hate. There would be nothing given to a rebellion that killed his very son."

"And he would have to know about it, and know how it happened, for that to happen. If, however, the son died heroically in battle, leading his makeshift band of fighters..." Bill shrugged.

"Don't do it Bill," Sam implored. "You know that it isn't right."

"He isn't going to change, Sam. You know that must as well as I do."

Sam looked back at the Belmarch camp, sickened by the sight of Bill. "I know that men have done wrong for generations."

"Don't get preachy with me."

Sam turned back, eyes flashing. "And I know men have changed. Even though all the world thinks they won't."

Bill held up his hands. "I can see you're angry. Save it for tonight, save it for them." He pointed to the Belmarch.

The sunset had started, casting colors of red, gold, and orange upon the puffy, swollen clouds in the west. The bottom of the sun had touched the tops of the trees, and was nearly to the horizon.

Part of him was right. Sam should save his strength for tonight. He looked down at his emaciated body and spindly arms. The vitality of life he had known when he first arrived had vanish, taken like a mist before the sun.

"We'll talk about this later," Sam said, smothering his rage and anger, not just at Bill, but at everything. He had to put the thing back to sleep, keep it from hurting anyone else.

"I'll go get the others," Bill said, giving him a funny look and then disappearing down the steps.

Sam looked one last time over the Golden River, reflecting the glory of the sunset. A star shone in the north, a reminder of the worlds that lay far away from their reach.

He took a deep, ragged breath, and gathered his strength. They would have only one night. They would have only one chance.

Sam turned back to the castle, and the task at hand.

25

ACTION IN THE NIGHT

They waited for the blanket of night to be complete before the men streamed out of the Keep. All of them were awake, all of them engaged in some form of activity.

Stars twinkled above them, a nearly full moon glowing and shedding light upon the castle. Sam worried about it. It was so bright he could make out the men standing next to them and the expressions they wore.

It was so bright the Belmarch might see them, and decide to investigate.

The group of men split into two. Bill took the majority of the masons to the wall, while Sam led the rest up to the unfinished tower and the waiting carpenters.

"Ready?" Kerien asked.

"Yes." Sam pulled out his hammer and got to work with the rest of them. He knocked free the final pegs holding the jib beam of the crane. The men holding it lowered it gently to the stone.

"Quietly," Sam said as they dropped it with a louder thunk than he wanted. "Your lives depend on it."

The rebuke did its job, and the silence that reigned among them was solemn and sacred. There was a tension in the air. Men looked over their shoulder at the Belmarch fires glowing

185

outside their former homes, and twitched if anyone made more than a small noise.

One of the masons assigned to their group was struggling with the rope and a knot. Sam went over to him and laid a hand on his shoulder. He looked up, a look of fear on his face.

Sam knelt beside him, taking the tension on the rope and giving him some slack. "Deep breath."

The man followed his advice, and was able to loosen the knot free. There was no wind, but the night was getting cold. Sam's breath came out in streams, and steam rose from the men as they worked.

Pieces came off the crane. Not as fast as he'd like, but fast enough. Soon men were taking them down the stairs, some too heavy for one man to take and some lighter.

The jib beam they left for last, set off to the side. As the heaviest piece of wood, it was the last to go.

Sam and five other men surrounded it. "Up to the stomach first, then the shoulder, just like we talked about."

They nodded, each one ready. Sam gave the order, and they knelt down and picked it up. It was heavy enough to take his breath away, but with all of them they soon had it onto their shoulders.

A man waiting farther down the stairs lit his candle, and they started down. It was too important and heavy to try and do without light, and it helped Sam see.

He led it down the spiral staircase, keeping the front of it as close to the wall as possible. It was long, almost too long, and he remembered the problems they had bringing it up.

After a few rests they made it to the door at the bottom. More men waited, and took positions on the jib beam, easing the strain on his shoulder. His legs were burning now.

But now they were to the first test of the night.

The door stood open, but its frame was small.

"Turn it down, and aim for the bottom left corner." Sam tried to move the beam into position, but either because he wasn't clear or they didn't know what to do it wasn't working.

"Bring it down," Sam said.

"We're trying." He looked back. Arms were in the air, but they couldn't raise it far enough up.

Sam crouched down instead, lowering his end and tipping it forward. The front of the jib scraped against the ground and the wall behind him.

he moved forward, pulling the beam with him. The front of it wobbled, moving precariously.

An inch more and they were at the threshold of the door, but the beam stuck on the inside of the jamb.

"Back up. Forward now." Sam shifted his shoulder, pulling it right. Then, the tip was through and into the hall.

Sam breathed a sigh of relief, stopping to take a rest with everyone else in the hallway. They took it through the castle with no other problems, soon coming into the yard with the night sky up above.

The cold was biting now. Sam's fingers were cold, colder than they had been. Other men had the tips of theirs turn black, losing all feeling in them.

They tramped across the courtyard and up the stairs of the wall. The others were standing by as the masons were disassembling the merlons, about a quarter of the way down each one.

This was the part that Sam was nervous about. The stones had to be taken off one by one, lest they drop the whole merlon into the rocks below.

"Are you sure this is the best way?" Ned asked, taking up a position next to him.

"Bill thought it was the quietest." It certainly was the slowest method.

Sam wondered why, but a few minutes watching them made it clear to see. The stones were subjected to the wind and the coldest part of the night, and it was difficult for the masons to work with them.

Even with hands covered in clothe they had to keep taking turns. It seemed like with each stone they removed another mason took a turn.

It was slow, agonizing going. The moon rose higher into the night sky.

Sam huddled with the others, keeping close to share each other's body heat. He wanted to yell at them, urge them on, but he knew that would only make things worse.

He couldn't work the hammer and chisels with the skill that they did, and had to keep watching helplessly. Bit by bit the merlons came down.

And bit by bit the masons' slowed down. The breathing became labored, even when they were resting. Sam wanted to help them, but couldn't.

Their movements grew more erratic. Chisels slipped, hammers rang against the stone instead of the chisel heads, and stones clattered to the battlement floor.

Sam winced at each one, but he couldn't stop them now. They were running out of time.

Then, he watched with horror as a young mason wen tot remove a stone, and accidentally knocked it over the edge of the wall.

26

A LETTER

Evan woke, a gentle tapping on his door. The night was cold outside his generous covers, and for a moment he almost went back to sleep.

Then, memories of the day before came to him, and his eyes were open.

"Come in."

Rhys entered, fully clothed with a makeshift pack in his hand. Evan threw off his covers and sat up, dangling his legs just above the ground.

He hadn't got much sleep, and a fog seeped through his brain. He had spent too much time last night thinking, unable to fall asleep.

"It looks like tonight is it then."

"They are finishing up the crane as we speak," Rhys said. There was a weight over his head, Evan could see it. This was not going to be an easy day.

"I've thought about this. No matter how I look at it you are the best choice." Evan pulled on a shirt, helping to keep the cold off his goose-bump ridden skin.

The room was musty. He didn't remember the last time it had been cleaned properly. Even his clothes had some of the smell on them. He should have asked for them to be washed, but until now it had slipped his mind.

He had so much more to think about lately.

"What will happen to me?" Evan asked.

"Only you will be able to answer that question," Rhys said.

"And if I go out now, to see you off?"

Rhys shifted his weight, but didn't say anything. Evan suspected as much.

It wasn't fair, he thought at first. But, having thought about it, he wasn't sure he would do anything different. They deserved someone who could lead.

"And what about Sam? Would he let them..."

"I suspect not. It seems I was wrong about him. He has more backbone than I expected." Rhys pulled his pack in front of him and rummaged through it. "But let's turn to happier things, shall we? I didn't come here just to say goodbye."

Evan asked for a moment to get dressed, and Rhys obliged by going into his study. He took some time to do it, selecting the uniform of the Hornblood line.

Before he put it on he stared at it. Evan had seen his father in it too many times to count. It was his standard wear, even though he did wear other outfits on occasion.

And now Evan was putting it on, perhaps for the last time. What would his father think of him? What would his father do in his situation?

He had grappled with it most of the night, but couldn't see any better option. This was his castle, this was his duty. He couldn't let it fall to others to shoulder the responsibility.

He had allowed that to happen for far too long.

The Overseer was waiting. Evan let out a wry chuckle at that. In a few hours he wouldn't be the Overseer anymore. That too would fall on his shoulders.

The undershirt was rough, and cold from sitting out all night. It scraped against his skin as it went over his head. The pants were no better.

Each successive layer added more cloth, and more weight. When he clicked the belt together, the sound echoing in the empty room.

It was done. He only had to add the coat and he was ready to leave his apartments.

Evan walked into his study directly. Rhys was waiting patiently and Evan bit him to sit.

"Thank you." He had something in his grip, but it was hidden in his pack.

"Before you go, I would like you to take a message." Evan joined him, sitting across from hi at his desk. The parchment he had been working on all night was still out, a pen and inkwell ready to be unstopped for the final touch.

"Certainly. Two whom?"

"To my father." Evan felt a wave of emotion. Fear, anger, sadness, desire. He fought it down. This might be the last time and the last chance to speak with him. "I've tried to detail what I've done here. And what I haven't."

He picked up the pen, the feather of it tickling his hand. Rhys was silent, and reverent. Why Evan unstopped the ink Rhys lit a candle for him to see.

"Thank you." The tip dipped into the black liquid, and it pulled as he brought it back to. A few drips came off and rippled the surface.

No more waiting. There wasn't anything else he had to add at this point, even through the struggling and the pain of the previous night.

The pen scratched against the parchment as he signed his name. He pulled it out of himself, and looked away as soon as he could.

A sweep of sand, a quick shake, and he rolled it up. A few drips of wax from the candle sealed it, and his ring left its imprint.

The Tree of Everling. *May the curse be lifted.*

Evan held out the roll, and Rhys took it carefully. "I will do everything in my power to make sure it gets to him."

Evan let go.

He took a deep breath. He had done wrong for so long there was no way to make up for it.

But he could try.

Rhys put the message away, and in return pulled out a small, red book. "I've had this for many years. It is fitting it falls to you."

Evan took it. The cover was soft, some sort of velvet. He dragged his thumb across it.

"Wait until I'm gone to read it," Rhys said. The darkness was overwhelming, but Evan knew the sun would come soon.

Rhys stood, and Evan followed. "It is time."

It was time. Evan knew it. He went around the desk, and grasped Rhys' hand.

"Go with the blessing of the Duke, and the fate of the castle

27

THE CRANE

Sam watched in horror as the mason grabbed for the rock and missed. The few moments it was falling felt like an eternity.A nd then it hit, clattering against the rocks below until it finally splashed into the river with a resounding plunk.

Bill was on the young man in an instant, beating him across the head. "Fool, you've ruined us all."

Sam was there, struggling to pull him off. The mason was whimpering and crying, blood trickling from cuts on his lip and the corner of his eye. "Bill, calm."

Bill almost turned on Sam, but he regained his composure and stopped. Everyone froze then, turning to the south.

Sam felt his heart beating fast, and blood was in his ears. He felt hot and sick. This was it. This was the end."We must move faster," Sam said in a whisper. "Set up the crane, now."

That sent them into action. The masons returned to their work, trying to take out the last remaining courses as quickly as they could."The next person to drop a rock over the side is going after it," Bill said. The warning didn't need the ominous growl he added, but it certainly cemented his seriousness.

"Bring over the braces, work around the others." Sam took one, setting it into the space they had made in the top of the wall. The other carpenters led the rest of the work.

193

Cold mist curled from his mouth. Sam hoped the Belmarch hadn't noticed or heard, but he knew they probably wouldn't miss it. The sound still rang in his own ears.

"Trent," Sam said as soon as he was done with a brace. Trent was at his side in a flash. "Warn the sentries. Get them ready for an attack, and make sure they have enough bows."

Trent nodded and then was gone. They still had to assemble the crane, and dawn wasn't far off. *We aren't going to make it.* The masons, as fast as they were going, were too slow.

"Bill, can we get away with not having to take them all down?" Sam pulled him off to the side.

Bill examined the wall, then looked back down at the boat. "With the swing of the crane, I don't think we can. We'll need to take them down to the floor."

Off in the distance, a drumbeat sounded. Bill cursed, and Sam couldn't help but do the same.

"We're out of time.""I'll knock them over," Bill said, picking up his hammer and pushing a mason out of the way.

Sam let him work, turning his attention to the crane. He knocked pegs into place, urging the others to work faster.

Kerien was supplying the parts as fast as he could. There was an urgency in everyone's actions that hadn't been there before.

Sam caught movement out of the corner of his eye. Forms were spilling out of the Keep. It was the women and children— all the men were already engaged with the wall work.

"Can they help?" Ned asked, seeing him looking."Have them ready to tie up the boat." Sam looked to the horizon. The sky was lightening.

And the Belmarch were assembling. Sam could hear their shouts carrying from their camp, helped by the calm stillness that still hung in the air.

Men were sweating and grunting. Hammers knocked and chipped away.

A loud crash behind him made him jump. Bill had cut loose a merlon, and it had crashed into the rocks below. He moved on to the next one. Four more to go, and two of them were already almost disassembled.

They might get away with it if they could get the crane assembled. Precious moments slipped by as the wooden structure took its form, a skeleton in the pre-dawn light.

They were able to work faster, though, with the lighter sky. "Careful, a mistake now will cost us dearly," Sam said as a hammer accidentally hit the frame instead of the peg it was aimed at.

They were down to the jib now, but they were going to have trouble raising it and keeping out of the masons' way.

Bill sent another pile of rock into the river and moved to the next. He worked like a machine, cutting away the bottom mortar joints as deep as he could get them. Every so often, he urged the others to push it off, judging his progress by how much it moved.

Sam was seated now, and he was so tired. His fingers were clumsy, and he noted how discolored they looked.

They rang the bell. There was no use trying to hide it now. The Belmarch knew, and they were coming.

Sam wished they could have tied up the boat earlier, had it ready for the crane, but they needed it built before they could loop the rope through the pulley.

"Pick it up from the right side. We'll come in through the top." Sam crouched next to it, fingers scraping against the stone-covered rock of the battlement. Together they lifted the beam.

It wobbled, off-balance from the awkward loading position. "Hold fast," Sam yelled, feeling it tip.

Bill dropped his hammer and was on the other side in an instant. The beam righted, then they pushed it into place. Kerien was at the peg, slamming it home.

Sam stood back to catch his breath, muscles drained and energy gone from the effort. Defenders had taken up their positions on the south wall, bows strung and arrows at the ready.

The Belmarch streamed across the plain in a disorganized rush.

But the rope was through and fed down to the men and women waiting at the boat below. The Overseer was helping, tying it up in a four-pointed harness Sam had never seen.

The crane was finished, the boat almost at the ready. Only two merlons remained.

But the Belmarch were coming.

28

THE EASTERN WALL

The soft peals of the bell echoed in his study. Evan opened his eyes and took a deep breath.

On the outside he may have appeared calm, but beneath he was a roil of conflicting thoughts and emotions. There was no better time than now.

He stood, clipped on his sword, and adjusted his uniform. People were shouting outside as he swung on his coat, buckling it beneath his chin.

His helmet lay on the desk. Evan looked at the crest of the Hornbloods and said a small prayer to his ancestors to give him strength.

He took it up and left. The corridors of the Keep were silent. His footsteps echoed as he walked the halls for the first time in weeks—perhaps months.

On the other side of each door, he expected to see someone waiting with a sword or a dagger, but with each door he passed, there was no one.

The Keep was empty.

Soon he was at the entrance doors, and he stopped before them. Cold crept in from the cracks between them and at the jambs, and some light.

Evan put his hand on the door, the rough wood cold beneath his fingers. The smell of outside drifted to him—a strange and intoxicating smell.

He was filled with fear, but he pushed open the door anyway.

Light stung his eyes, and Evan blinked back tears that welled up from the cold that stung them.

The courtyard was a chaos of action, most of it at the eastern wall. Men were shooting arrows on the south battlements, some flying back in return.

When he caught his breath and bearings, Evan examined the situation with a pounding heart rate.

Men were struggling with ropes and a boat by the eastern wall. *That would be the responsibility of the Overseer*. The south wall, however, looked like it could use some help.

The men on it were disorganized, guards were yelling and shouting. Evan's feet seemed frozen in place. He couldn't move.

He felt the presence of Yand at his back. Silent, imposing, always looking on and judging him without showing it.

Evan mustered his courage, swallowed his fear, and walked to the southern wall.

Sam couldn't believe his eyes. There he was, the Duke of Hornblood walking across the courtyard. He didn't run, he didn't falter, but he walked with a purpose Sam didn't expect.

"Sam," Ned said, breaking his concentration. He had one hand on the rope, and realized that he needed to focus. With one last look he turned back to the task at hand.

Another crash, and a cheer from everyone on the wall. Another merlon had seen its demise in the river.

And only two more remained.

Kerien was wrapping the rope around the pulley, and Sam helped feed the slack through.

Below them the ropes tightened as they pulled the ropes up. A large knot lifted into the air, then the slack was gone.

Ned hammered the final pin in place.

"Pull," Sam bellowed, pushing his shoulder into the capstan. It didn't move, but more men threw their weight behind it, until at last it lifted with a creak.

Shouts from below cheered them on. The boat tipped and wobbled, but then was in the air. It broke free of the snow that had piled up on it and swung.

The Overseer was running up the stairs, and reached them as the boat did. Hands grabbed and pulled at it, swinging it over the wall.

The crane stuck, lodged on some projection. Sam called for a halt, and they pushed the boat back far enough for Kerien to smash the offending bit of wood free.

"Get in," Sam said. Rhys, with the help of a few people boosting him, climbed into the boat.

There was still one merlon in the way. Bill was yelling, and more than a few masons were chipping at the base of it.

Sam pulled at the boat with the others, and it swung back over the middle of the wall. They held it there, giving the masons enough room to work without getting in their way.

There were Belmarch soldiers at the eastern wall now. Sam could see the archers leaning out over the wall and firing at them.

A man was hit by a Belmarch arrow and tumbled off with a scream. Sam winced when the sound was cut short.

"Bill, you need to hurry." They hadn't come around the eastern wall yet, and Sam wondered what they were seeing and thinking.

Could they see the boat from their vantage point? They had to have seen it, otherwise they wouldn't be attacking.

The snow had slowed them down. The first rays of the sun were striking the cloudy sky. Sunrise dawned on the castle.

And still the boat sat, waiting to break free from the wall. Sam checked the distance again, careful up against the now open wall.

It will make it. His heart fluttered and his head spun. Sam leaned up against the frame of the crane and waited.

29

ATTACK OF THE BELMARCH

The stairs were icy and slippery, but Evan took little time to mount them. He kept his head up, his gaze fixed to the top.

The defenders on the wall were still in organized chaos. Bowstrings twanged all around as Evan got to the top, men shouting for cover and pointing out where the enemy had gone.

For a second Evan stood helpless at the top of the stairs. Then, someone noticed him, taken aback.

The man's mouth dropped open, and his eyes widened. "D-Duke," he stammered.

The words caught the attention of others, and the surprise spread like a ripple in a pond, disrupting the defenders from shooting arrows.

There was a bow leaning up against the side of the wall. Evan walked over and took it, testing its strength. It had been a while since he had shot one, but he picked up an arrow and nocked it to the string.

His coat was in the way, so he pushed it off to the side and leaned over the edge of the wall.

Attackers swarmed up the plain to the wall carrying ladders, but there were only a few of them.

Evan pulled the bow back, struggling against the weight of it, and set the feather of the arrow against his cheek. It tickled his skin, but he ignored it as he sighted down the bow.

He released. The arrow flew with a whisper, finally striking the leg of an attacker.

Evan frowned and turned back to the others. Men were staring at him. Some had looks of horror, most of surprise, and there were some hard looks of anger spread among them.

"We must buy them time." Evan picked up another arrow. "Keep them from the east wall."

Evan turned back to the attackers, feeling a pricking in between his shoulder blades. This was the critical moment, and his stomach turned knots with fear.

He didn't want to die, if he could help it, and the thought of his death at the hands of his own subjects made him squirm even more.

"You heard him," a guardsman said. "Keep them busy." Men responded, and turned back to their defense.

Evan sighted, then let fly. This time his aim was better, taking a man in the chest. Around him the others fired on the lead attackers, trying to keep them from rounding the corner of the wall.

Evan looked back to the boat. It was dangling precariously over the wall. He hoped they had enough time, but turned his attention back to the attackers.

He would buy them as much time as he could.

A crack rang out. "Push it!" Bill screamed. They pushed with all their might.

It gave.

The stones crashed to the ground, and the way was clear.

Sam's heart soared with hope. "Hold on Rhys." He leaned against the boat, urging the others to do the same.

As it swung, slowly, Sam caught sight of Belmarch attackers rounding the corner of the east wall.

The defenders were trying to stop them, throwing down arrows and stones. Duke Hornblood was in the lead, hair disheveled and looking harried, pouring on as much damage as he could.

The Overseer was clutching the edges of the boat, leaning over.

"Lower him down!" Sam pulled at the capstan brake, letting it free. The weight of the boat helped them, and the rope sang out as it fell.

"That's too fast, slow it!"

Hands grabbed at the rope, then let go as they burned. Sam couldn't feel his fingers, but clutched at it.

He feared it wasn't enough.

The boat hit the water with a wrenching crash, waves spreading out from its sides and splashing up the rocks.

Sam dashed to the edge, examining their work.

His heart soared. It was in the river, caught by the current.

Overseer Rhys was sawing at the ropes. He cut the boat free and took up the oar, pushing the prow of it further into the river.

But the Belmarch were close enough to fire on him now, and were sending arrows his way.

"Stop them, we must stop them!" Duke Hornblood was calling to all of them.

It spurned them to action. All the men on the wall rushed to help, picking up stones and blocks and anything they could get their hands on.

Arrows and rock rained down from the wall, falling upon the attackers like rain.

They wilted from the attack, and seeing the boat was too far into the water, they fell back, slipping and sliding over the blood covered snow.

Sam's heart thumped, and a lump formed in his throat. Tears formed in his eyes and fell. They had done it.

A cheer rang out from the wall, and the defenders shouted and whooped as the Belmarch ran out of bowshot and back to their camp.

They left more than a few bodies behind them, and even more limping, injured by the failed attack.

Sam watched Overseer Rhys paddle out to the center of the river. He held up a hand to signal he was unharmed. Behind him the dawn exploded in a cacophony of color.

They had a chance. It was a small one, but it was still a chance.

Sam leaned on the ruins of the wall and watched the sunrise, hope blossoming in his heart.

Epilogue

Evan gulped down the fresh winter air, trying to recover. Cheers surrounded him, but he could not partake in their joy.

Rhys was gone now, a speck that had disappeared on the river downstream. He felt some of his fear go with him, but not all of it.

When his heart had calmed and the cheers had died down Evan still faced the river, afraid to turn and face his subjects.

But face them he must.

Squaring his shoulders he turned. Eyes stared at him, all faces turned his direction. Sweat trickled down his brow and he wiped it away, but it wasn't sweat. It was blood.

He felt the wound. It was a graze, from an arrow, most likely. He didn't remember how he had gotten it, but it didn't matter now.

Evan was near the edge of the wall and suddenly became extremely aware of it. Forty men faced him. All it would take was one little push. They could claim it was an accident.

"You did well today," Evan said. He wasn't sure what else he could say. "I haven't..." he trailed off.

The wall was silent. Evan lowered his head. "I like to think I'm a different man than I was."

Sam Freeman was before him then, ripping a strip of his own ragged coat off. "You're hurt, Your Highness."

"I don't deserve that title."

"Deserve it or not, we'll get you patched up." Sam turned back to the others. "Isn't that right?"

Murmurs ran through the crowd, but there wasn't the same hostility Evan had known before. He let Sam wrap his head.

"Thank you," Evan said.

Sam smiled. "You are welcome. On a day like today, we should celebrate." Sam turned back to the crowd. "This day we will remember to our last breath."

They cheered again, smiles appearing on faces. Evan wasn't sure if he was out of danger, but he knew that he was safe then.

He couldn't help but smile.

EXCERPT FROM BRANCH OF THE EVERLONG: EPIC OF HORNBLOOD CASTLE #3

Scritch, scratch. Little legs pattered by in the darkness. Sam waited patiently, even though his mind was telling him to move.

Small squeaks echoed in the room, the dark hollows of the castle basement.

It was getting closer. It scuffed and shuffled. He smelled horrible, covered in refuse and his unwashed scent from weeks of the same clothes and no chance to get them clean.

Behind the creature water dripped in a slow, steady flow. His belly gnawed at his ribcage, almost on fire.

He had to wait.

It got closer, and then it was there. Sam lunged.

The rat tried to move, but his blade found it faster. Red, glowing eyes stared at him as it hissed and spat, trying to scratch him.

He was breathing hard, even though he hadn't moved more than a foot. This was a big one, and he was pleased.

The movements died, the screams of the rat slowing and then dying away.

Sam panted in the darkness. Warm blood covered his hand. He pulled his prey up and slung it over his shoulder.

Up the stairs he climbed, one foot in front of the other. Like every day he wondered whether Rhys had made it. Not knowing ate at him more than the hunger.

He stopped at the top of the stairs to catch his breath and slow his pounding heart, leaning against the cold, hard wall.

Sam put his head against it, letting the rough, cool stone suck the heat from his head, and coughed.

It was a dry, rasping cough. His leg throbbed, the old wounds coming back to him. When he had recovered enough, he opened the door.

Blinking against the light, Sam stepped out of the dungeons of the Keep and into the hall. He was still inside, but light trickled in from the rooms up ahead.

Voices drifted in, and he shuffled to them. He took a look at his blood-drenched hand, already drying off, and thought about washing.

He winced, thinking of the freezing cold water against his skin. That they still had plenty of, if they could break the ice off the top of the well.

"Sam!" Martha exclaimed, cutting off her conversation with Belinda. "What happened to you?"

"I've killed the thing eating our food." Sam dropped the rat on the counter. Its tongue rolled out of its mouth, but the rest of it was going stiff. "I know it isn't appetizing, but I thought we could eat it. I thought it fitting."

He slumped into a chair. So little strength, there was too little of it left in his body. He eyed the rat, thinking of how its flesh might taste.

Warm and succulent, roasted over a nice, crackling fire. Dripping with fat. Sam's mouth watered.

"I'll do what I can," Martha said.

Belinda was staring at him, a hint of a glare subdued by her exhaustion.

"Give it to the boy," Sam said. He was getting so thin it broke his heart every time he saw those little cheeks.

Beady little eyes poked out from the blanket at her chest. He moved, coughed, then started crying.

Belinda turned and comforted him, rocking him back and forth and shushing him. She shot him one last glare and walked out of the kitchen.

The rat wouldn't last. They would eat of all it, that he knew for sure, down to cracking the bones to get to the marrow. They needed the meat.

He felt a wave of sadness wash over him that this is what it had come to. Sam tried to control it, but he was so tired.

How long has it been since Rhys left in the boat? It was all a haze now, the fog that never left his brain seeping through his body.

Sam sniffed. He averted his gaze, aware that Belinda didn't take too kindly to him. His heart ached at that too, wished he could do something about it, but he knew that her sadness and grief overruled everything else. She had gone so long with hate in her that he wasn't sure it would ever go away.

And that ate at him too, gnawing worse than the hunger did.

He wanted to make it go away but knew that she was in total control of the situation.

"That is... kind of you," Martha said, snapping him out of his thoughts and back to reality.

"I hate to see him like that. He should be fat and happy, not sticks and bones poking through his skin." His own skin felt tight, as he suspected everyone else's did. Fat was in short supply within the walls of the castle.

"I'll see what I can do about cooking it." Martha stared at the dead rat. She pushed up her sleeves and took out a knife, sharpening it with quick, efficient strokes, only expending enough energy to get it sharp enough to slice underneath the matted fur and skin, parting it from the muscle with quick slices.

"I can bring you something to burn." There wasn't much left, but he could find scraps to use. A few sticks might do for a fire. His mouth watered just watching her cut the measly strips of meat from the tiny bones.

A few moments of work and the rat was dressed and ready to eat, organs and all. "I'll put it into a stew." Martha looked around and pulled out a small pot. "This will do."

Sam eased himself into the corner, sliding down the stone until he was supported by the floor. It was cold too, no way to escape it. The smell of the rat, blood and bone and meat, drifted over to him and tortured him. His breath was coming in short gasps. "Let me rest, and then I will go out to the workshop."

His eyelids felt heavy and tried to drift shut, but he didn't let them. After a few minutes, and while Martha prepared everything, his breathing steadied, and Sam got back to his feet. He nodded in her direction and walked out to the workshop, bracing himself for the cold before opening the Keep door and walking out into the snow and wind.

It wasn't as cold as it had been, but it was still brutal on his body. He was shivering within a few seconds, and his hands fumbled when he finally reached the workshop and pulled out the smallest scraps of wood he could. The wood pile was down to almost nothing. They had burned almost everything else and were scavenging beams from the castle when they had the strength at the beginning of the day.

He couldn't get Archie's face out of his mind as he worked, and the faces of all the others that had died. They walked in a long, sad line through his mind, just staring at him. It was enough, and he felt a mixture of shame and sadness as they did.

After that, and while he walked back to the Keep, came the worst of it. The children, emaciated and thin, still living, but only just, came to mind. He wanted to close his eyes when he got inside but didn't. A few of them peered out at him from the pile of bodies, watching him cross the room with curiosity until he slipped out of view and down the hall.

They were all counting on him to survive, and there was nothing he could do about it now. Their fate rested with Overseer Rhys and his luck, for better or for ill.

"This is all I could find that was handy," Sam said as he entered the kitchen. Martha looked at it with tired eyes and nodded. He got to work lighting the fire under the pot, a strange sight in a fireplace so large to be confined to such as small fire. They could have thrown in a quarter of the tree and burned it, and probably would in the future.

If they survived.

The fire caught, and smoke filled the kitchen. The tiny amount of heat coming from it was a blessing, and Martha pressed up beside him to share in it. Soon they had a small fire, and the pot pressed against it.

She was so close, and warm. *It feels nice, in a way*. That strange fluttering feeling came back in his stomach, pushing aside the hunger for a few blessed moments.

He knew he should say something, but he wasn't sure what. He was keenly aware of every part of her touching him. She moved, reaching out a hand to stir the pot with a long spoon. That side of his body was chilled, used to the warmth of her skin, wrapped up in all the clothing she could find.

Sam cleared his throat. "What do you think we will do in spring?"

Martha looked at him. A lock of her hair fell down over her eye. "What do you mean by that question?"

"I'm not sure." Sam looked away. "Trying to pass the time, I imagine."

"I pray that we make it to spring." He looked back at her, but she was staring at the fire. It was dancing, sending up small tufts of smoke that curled up the chimney. Sam wanted to reach down and hold it in his hand, bring it near to his bosom to suck up its warmth, but he restrained himself and savored the momentary feeling of warmth it gave him, little as it may be. "I'm afraid the food will be gone next week."

He knew it was coming, but it still hit him in the stomach like a punch to the gut. All their rationing and scrimping, all of it was for nothing. "It will run out when it runs out. We'll have to go on after that."

"Until when? When we die?" She had tears in the corner of her eyes. "The children..."

"If there was anything you could do for them you would have done it already." Martha bit her thumb and squeezed her eyes shut. She looked so vulnerable, so frail.

Sam wanted to reach out and take her hand, sweep her into his arms and hold her. For all her iron appearance, her harsh way with the other girls in the castle, this was another side that he had never seen.

A breeze from the window gusted through the kitchen and the fire sputtered dangerously. Sam reached out his hands to shield it. The pot hadn't boiled yet.

What am I supposed to say, what am I supposed to do? Sam chewed at his lip. Martha wiped her eyes.

"Here I am blubbering when there's a job to do." She stirred the pot again. "What must you think of me?"

"I think you care about everyone around you." Sam swallowed. "I... admire you for it."

Their eyes locked. Sam felt his face flush, steam rising to his cheeks. Martha was searching his eyes, looking for something, but he wasn't sure what. "The soup is ready."

His heart was pounding. He could still feel the heat from her body on him, but it was gone an instant later when she stood and took the pot from the fire. It had been boiling. For how long, he wasn't sure, but the fire was dying down and the wood had been almost all consumed.

"Did I say something wrong?" Sam stood too.

"Will you get Belinda for me?" Martha poured the soup into waiting bowls. She refused to make eye contact with him, but worked with a steady, practiced hand.

His mind was a rush of emotions and thoughts tripping over each other. What had he said to make her act this way? Was it him saying she cared about everyone? *I can't see why that would make her angry.*

All he could do was turn and leave, searching for Belinda and her child. He found her in the great hall, huddled up against the mass of bodies, and signaled for her.

The confusion was still in him, but there was also a strange sense of anger with it. It must have shown in his face, because Belinda looked at him with a soft expression of alarm and clutched her child closer. Still, she followed him into the hall, away from the others.

"What is it? What have I done?" she asked when they were out of earshot of the others, in a hissing whisper.

"You've done? Nothing you've done." Sam took a deep breath, calmed himself. "I'm sorry, it's just...you wouldn't understand."

"Hold on." Belinda had been following him, but at the words he turned to see her stopped. Gone was the expression of concern, now replaced with one of anger. "Have you hurt her?"

"Hurt who?" Sam took a step back and raised his hands.
"Martha. Have you broken her heart?"

Get Branch of the Everlong

ECLECTIC STORIES

Thank you for spending your precious time reading this book.

If stories make you salivate, learn more about lore, take an exclusive sneak peek behind the scenes, and get writing updates in my newsletter, Eric's Eclectic Stories.

As a bonus you'll get *Stories from the Deep*, a Patmos Sea Fantasy Adventure anthology that gives a glimpses of lore, extra prologues and epilogues, and character backstories.

If you aren't satisfied, unsubscribe at any time.

Join at erickercher.com.

-Eric Kercher

Also By Eric Kercher

Patmos Sea Fantasy Adventure Series

*Fathomless Pursuit - Architect's Prize - Ironbound Path
Sunken Prey – Unanswered Prophecy – Hardened Pilgrim –
Final Peace*

Seventh Hall Chronicles

Seventh Hall - Ode to the Survivors - Bastion of the Deep

Epic of Hornblood Castle

*Siege of the Unfinished Keep – Winter at Hornblood – Branch
of the Everlong*

Castlebound Adventures

Rats in the Cellar!- Save the Cat!

Collections

Red Eagle Anthology – Searchlight Anthology

Stand Alone

Planet Reaping – Dukedom Rumble – Savage Space Salvage

About Author

Eric Kercher was born and raised in a small town on the Great Plains on good books. After attending a small state school on the east coast he joined the US Navy to serve his country and explore the world. He worked on submarines, and the world beneath the waves captivated him with all its mysteries and wonders. After spending time in larger cities, he's settled down in a quiet town with his wife and children. When not on an adventure in a good book the author enjoys creating dust woodworking, architecture, and spending time with loved ones.

Find out more at www.erickercher.com.